£2

Mrs Liza C
% 7. Merchis
Edinburgh. EH10 4RX

D0512849

SURVIVING ADOLESCENCE

SURVIVING ADOLESCENCE
A handbook for adolescents
and their parents

PETER BRUGGEN
MB, ChB, DRCOG, DCH, FRCPsych
Consultant Psychiatrist, Hill End Adolescent Unit,
Hill End Hospital, St Albans, Hertfordshire

and

CHARLES O'BRIAN
CQSW, DSW, CRCC
Senior Lecturer in Social Work, Oxford Polytechnic

faber and faber

LONDON · BOSTON

First published in 1986
by Faber and Faber Limited
3 Queen Square, London WC1N 3AU

Typeset by Goodfellow & Egan Ltd, Cambridge
Printed in Great Britain by
Redwood Burn Ltd, Trowbridge, Wiltshire
All rights reserved

British Library Cataloguing in Publication Data

Bruggen, Peter
Surviving adolescence.
1. Adolescence
I. Title   II. O'Brian, Charles
305.2'35   HQ796
ISBN 0-571-13936-1

Library of Congress Cataloging-in-Publication Data

Bruggen, Peter.
Surviving adolescence.
(Faber paperback)
Summary: Explores such problems of adolescence as
drugs, sex, dealing with parents, coping with
physical and emotional development, and achieving
increasing independence.
1. Adolescence.   2. Adolescent psychology.
3. Puberty.   [1. Adolescence]   I. O'Brian, Charles.
II. Title
HQ796.B758   1986   305.2'35   86-2159
ISBN 0-571-13936-1 (pbk.)

Contents

CONTENTS

Acknowledgements

To the many families, including our own, who told us what to do.

To Kathryn Redway, who taught us how to give form to our creativity.

To Maureen Jack, who produced the manuscripts.

I

Introduction and Overview

Adolescents grow up. But it is fairly common, in fact inevitable, that many issues that are either resolved or unresolved in adolescence have reverberations throughout adult life. A social influence in adolescence, such as schooling, might affect future career prospects in later adult life. What is happening in society in its wider context, such as rising unemployment, will have an effect on adolescents going into young adulthood and their chances of making their own lives. They may have to stay at home longer. This has obvious implications for parents as well.

Old age can be seen as a sort of adolescence too. There is a degree of losing control of one's life, becoming dependent, irascible and awkward, untidy, and thinking differently to others around you.

Very often it is the first sexual encounter that significantly affects the way people relate to others. The difference in ability to make relationships, from being rejected in the first instance to being accepted, is important.

The feelings you have in adolescence about reproduction are usually brought into fruition during adult life. Parents first start preparing for future parenthood while they are still adolescents.

Family life can be seen as a cycle: being born, childhood, adolescence, young adulthood, courtship and marriage, middle age, old age and death. We mention this because we wish to remind adolescents that they are part of a process that they are going through along with their parents and grandparents. And parents, we wish to remind you of this because you have gone through some of the stages and will be going through others. Do you realise that you are bringing up future grandparents?

We start by giving an overview of the subject about which we write. If you read this overview, you can decide what to do next. If you like it, you will want to read the rest of the book. If you do not like it, you may decide not to read any more or, that it is a medicine you do not like but which might still be of some use.

If we said that we should be upset if you did not read this book, you might recognise a ploy which you may yourself have used or had used against you and which you do not like.

If you have decided to stay with us, we hope that you will be reading and enjoying some alternative tactics for use when people, particularly in your family, do not do as you wish. We hope that these are a more creative way of getting through what can often be a very difficult time for everyone.

We do not know who you are, but you have read this line at least. We hope there are many of you and that you have come from all walks of life, that you will be interested in joining with us in a journey to see what adolescence is like. We hope that what you read in our book may stimulate you to think about your experiences and to develop change, whether you are an adolescent or an adult. At times we address you, parents, at times, you, adolescents. Either may eavesdrop.

Historical View

People have always complained about the younger generation. We shall not compete with those authors who appear to vie with each other to find the earliest reference to this. One saying, attributed to Oscar Wilde, is that the tragedy of youth is that it is wasted on the young.

Because there is now a more sophisticated awareness of initiation rites which have existed for generations in primitive tribes, paradoxically it may be harder to recognise these in contemporary society: the first drink in the pub, the first signing-on at the Job Centre, undergoing a three-year apprenticeship in a trade, sitting arduous A-level exams, these are some of today's initiation rites.

In the large families of previous generations children entering adolescence started to look after their younger brothers and sisters. Now, more often, they do it for money and it is called babysitting; although it is still not uncommon to find adolescents caring for their younger brothers and sisters while their mother does a part-time job.

Children have always worked and still do, although society through the years has had different reactions. The age at which full-time paid work is permitted by law has been gradually raised, and today we shudder when we think of child labour: we also protest about youth unemployment.

When Screaming Lord Sutch first campaigned in a British general election with his Raving Monster Loony Party, he advocated votes for 18-year-olds. People laughed at him. During his last campaign Lord Sutch was advocating votes for 16-year-olds. He was still being laughed at by many, including some 18-year-olds, who now have the vote.

At the time of writing, during the second term of a Conservative government, we do not know if the adolescents who were brought up under Labour Britain in the 1960s are the same who, once they had the vote, put the Conservative government into power in the 1980s. During the US presidential election of 1984, Ronald Reagan, a right-winger in his seventies, had the majority youth vote.

Some adolescents have always been actively involved in politics. Nowadays in the fighting in Iran, Northern Ireland and in the many guerrilla movements around the world, people as young as 12 are bearing arms. We have seen how the Red Guard in China brought a comparatively strong, well-established regime, which was itself 'revolutionary', to change. Adolescents are not involved in political movements to do with the Left only but also with the Right. The Hitler Youth in Nazi Germany and the National Front in modern Britain have had adolescents actively working to further their political aims. The strength of the adolescent presence cannot have been more vividly put than in the film version of the musical *Cabaret*. A young boy sings 'Tomorrow Belongs to Me' and, as the camera angle widens, his shoulders and the swastika of his Nazi uniform come into view.

A Definition of Adolescence

Our own view of adolescence is in terms of the relationship between the adolescent and other people, particularly adults. It is a process which is focused on a move from dependence to independence. Adolescence is a period of becoming independent while still remaining dependent. This is different from being a child almost wholly dependent on adults, different too from being an old person moving from independence to dependence.

Take the following:
1. A 17-year-old who is a member of the armed forces posted abroad
2. A 16-year-old about to take O-levels
3. A 14-year-old living in a foster home
4. An 18-year-old who is at university, but still living at home
5. An 18-year-old at university but living away from home
6. A 25-year-old who has completed his education, has good employment and still living at home
7. A 16-year-old who is living in a bedsit, on social security, because that brings him more money than living at home.

Which of the above would you call an adolescent? Using the state of dependence with the move to independence as a criterion you may see some of these people as adolescent and some as not. You could use the same criterion with people that you know. You might also think about how much the people you know are still dependent on others. Are they still surprised and angry when things do not turn out as they want? Do they carry on behaving as if they should? And if things do not, then do they see it all as somebody else's fault and nothing to do with them?

If adolescents are the ones who are still dependent then there must be others on whom they are dependent. So, now we turn to you, the parents.

When do you stop feeling responsible for your children and what they do? When do you stop feeling responsible for organising their day-to-day management? When do you stop buying their sanitary towels or checking that they clean their teeth?

But of course you are not alone or isolated in this because you as parents, and as adults, are dependent on other people for your sense of status. One of your status factors is being seen as a parent. That is, being accountable for your children, you are seen as the mother or father of your child. You are 'John's mother' or 'Jennifer's father'.

Colin, his father and their dentist

When Colin cancelled his appointment at the dentist's because he was too tired after work, his father was angry and worried about how this would affect his own relationship with the dentist. Would he, the father, be held to account and in some sense be blamed for his son's behaviour when he made his own next visit? Would it be taken out on him?

How much do you think that people around you, be they shopkeepers, milkmen or doctors, see your adolescent children as independent beings, or how much do you still see them as the product or responsibility of you, and still your charge? Do remember how doctors seem to want to be able to view and treat adolescents as independent beings. On the other hand the law does not recognise financial liability until the age of 18 and your children cannot in their own right take out hire purchase agreements until their eighteenth birthday. Until that time, parents can be held responsible for their children's debts.

When does Richard or Linda, stop being seen as your son or daughter?

Adolescence as a Pre-occupation

Do you remember when you last had a serious adult crisis? Perhaps it was a bereavement, when one of your parents died, or a sudden change in your marital relationship, a change or loss of job, or moving house. You will remember the over-riding pre-occupation of the event. More than just the anticipation a few days before a holiday when you start to think more and more about the journey. Far more than that. Perhaps you have forgotten for just how much of your own adolescence you may have been similarly preoccupied. The pre-occupation of the adolescent with adolescence can be just as pre-occupying as that of the adult going through a major life crisis. One of the things that causes difficulties is that the length of adolescence is much greater than the duration of most adult crises. Adolescents have this pre-occupation and do hate it if they feel that it is being trivialised by adults. Their concern for their spots, the shape of their figure or whether they have the right face, is very important to them. They are heavily influenced by pop idols, by their friendships and by the pressures of their own peer group. They have their almost secret signs of membership to their own group or their club. We can all remember codes on the backs of envelopes. For them to be told that they will grow out of it may be felt as an intense provocation.

They may resent any diversion from their internal pre-occupation. They may resent any attempt to blunt their ideas or to take their mind off what they are most pre-occupied with at the time. In some people's view adults may be inclined to do this because they may feel threatened by what is going on in the adolescents but more likely, we think, because they want to protect the adolescent from disillusionment too soon. We sometimes fear that this adult protection in itself becomes a self-fulfilling prophecy. That is, trying to protect adolescents from later disillusionment does cause a disillusionment in itself. The adults are not letting the adolescents face reality and find out for themselves.

The Changes

Adolescence is a change. Adolescence is about changes of many different sorts: physical, emotional, family, legal, group and social.

The steady increase in physical size and strength of the pre-adolescent years is replaced by a spurt. Girls first and then boys start to grow faster. Muscles become stronger and limbs heavier. Milk teeth are finally lost and permanent teeth are established. Skin becomes prone to acne and approaches its maximum ability to take grafts. Hair on the head changes in texture and in distribution. Facial hair starts to appear in boys and body hair in both boys and girls. Voice changes in both, but is more pronounced in boys. Features of the face may start to take on a characteristically male or female distribution and become more clearly defined. Body shape – the width of the hips, width of shoulders and shape of chest – becomes apparent. Menstruation and ejaculation start.

The hormonal counterpart is there too. Hormones are a sort of chemical communicator between different parts of the body and they influence bodily growth, change and feelings. They influence things such as how fast or far you grow, how soft or hard your skin is and how many spots you have, (that is just spots, not acne; do remember that acne is treatable), how thick your hair is and where it grows, and your sexual changes and feelings. They have an important part to play in regulating the menstrual cycle. The change in them is the physical counterpart of the changed state of arousal in adolescence.

The next big change in hormones occurs in pregnancy.

The emotional changes in adolescence may raise many issues for the child, including a sense of indignation at still being referred to as a child. In part these are a reaction to the physical changes taking place and are encompassed in the enquiry, 'What is happening to me?' The adolescent notices a change in size and strength and sexuality, that the range of feelings experienced may be wider, and that some take on a different intensity. Some things take on a new and great significance, while others that were important in childhood become less so.

Questions

Am I all right? Is it all right? Am I special? Am I the only one? Can I control this or is this controlling me? How long will it last? Do my parents know what will happen next? What shall I find out next? What am I discovering? What will it be like to have a period? What will it be like to ejaculate? What will it be like to have sex? What will it be like to be attractive? Shall I be attractive? Who will be my friend(s)?

Additional to all these emotional changes happening in every adolescent are the many developments in the relationships adolescents have with the people around. Foremost is their family, then their own friends, boys and girls. The different genders lose their positions as playmates and start to become objects of sexual attraction or conspiracy. Or, at the very least, members of the same age group may become objects of more intense sexual curiosity.

Adolescents start to create a distance from the family. They reach out for more independence and want to go out alone. They may wish to accompany their families less and less on family outings. Where to go on holiday becomes a great issue and whether they should take part or not.

There are a lot of changes to do with going to school. Approaching adolescence, or in adolescence itself, most young people change from primary to secondary school. Expectations about secondary schooling are built up long before they move. Which school will they go to? Will they be with people they know or will they have to get to know others? Does getting into what seems to be the 'best' school mean splitting up from friends? There may be positive or negative expectations – either way, a powerful pressure.

Once at secondary school, adolescents may decide to initiate change themselves. A wish by pupils to change school is not uncommon. They become more aware of the systems around them.

Adolescents become more aware of themselves in relation to society. They start to talk about politics, about laws, about the police, about the fairness and unfairness of society. They become interested in sports teams, in groups, popular music or religion. Although they may have been interested in these things as children, there is a qualitative difference in the intensity of feeling they now have about the very same subjects they supported as children.

Religion

Parents may have strong religious views and practices which their children do not share. Conversely, parents who are neutral, ambivalent or against active religious beliefs may find that their adolescent children start practising a faith.

Parents will be familiar with the proliferation of various religious organisations. Some of you may call all religions extreme, others may feel that some are part of the established order of things and that they have your approval. Other parents may be religious and feel that it is a major commitment for them.

If your children join religious orders of which you do not approve, what can you do? Some parents, once discussion has failed, have employed professionals to get their children back, physically, emotionally and ideologically. Others have learned to live with it.

We know of one adolescent whose parents objected to the firearm practice of the religious organisation he had joined. He said to them 'Would you have been so upset if I had joined the army?'

Law and Order

Adolescents become aware of the law and the law becomes aware of them. The law starts to recognise them as responsible for their actions and to have expectations about how adolescents behave. One way or another, the protection of children from having to face the consequences of their actions, ceases. Yet there are many confusions, ambiguities and contradictions.

The age of consent for heterosexual intercourse and male homosexual intercourse is different. The law does not recognise female homosexuality, and so the law cannot help girls to make a moral judgement.

Another way in which society presents adolescents with contradictions is by the practice of imposing solutions which are described as caring ones but are experienced by the adolescents themselves as punishments. When a court places a child into the care of the local authority under a care order is an example.

There is no law to stop an adolescent from smoking cigarettes, nor from buying them; but it is an offence for a vendor to sell them to someone under the age of 16. To the question from an adolescent of our acquaintance – 'If I buy cigarettes from a vending machine, is the law being broken?' – we have no answer. There are similar restrictions on the sale and consumption of alcohol in certain premises, and the deliberate selling of glue for the purposes of sniffing has become the subject of recent legislation.

The law is involved with other experiences of young people. They are not allowed to see some films until a certain age, although they may be old enough to act in them. Recent legislation about video nasties is especially directed at the supposed vulnerability of young people in the area of what they see and hear. Parents who censor what their youngsters may watch either on television or at the cinema may be encouraged by knowing that research has given us conclusive evidence of a direct and causal relationship between watching violence on the screen and actions. Of course, they may get into the cinema under age without your knowing. They may see a pornographic video at a friend's house. There are some things you do not know about or, knowing about, you cannot stop. This does not mean that you have to 'approve' by way of collusion.

It is after all obvious that advertising works for the organisations that spend many millions of pounds on making television commercials aimed directly at the young customer. Parliament is now taking the influence of video so seriously that for the first time the industry's own self-censors and the Home Secretary are being brought together.

Adolescents are old enough to join the army and be killed. While eligible to die for their country, they are not yet old enough to vote for the government that directs them. But their elders, the public, cry out when the armed forces send 17-year-olds to serve in Northern Ireland.

Of course there may seem little logic to the arbitrariness of the particular ages at which one thing becomes legal or another thing becomes obligatory. Since the Romans tried to do it, no one has really sat down with a fresh piece of paper to decide what should happen when; rather laws have arisen in response to pressures at particular times. It seems to us that there is always some degree of public discussion proposing change in one of three particular areas: the age of consent to sexual intercourse in girls, the age for the sale of alcohol and the age at which children should be allowed to leave school.

The Life Cycle

Families change: it is a misconception to see them as static. For there to be growth in the family there must be change. No adolescent gets three A-levels, becomes captain of the netball team or accepted for ballet school without changing. And when one person in the family changes it affects the others.

All families have rules of behaviour: the father goes out to work; the women do most of the cooking; the men do most of the physical maintenance of the house; one particular parent does most of the driving; one of the parents does more of the disciplining; the mother manages the finances; the child who is upset turns to the mother; the mother deals with the crying child in the middle of the night; people get up and go to bed in a certain order. We see rules as being 'geared' to change rather than to keeping things the same and we like to think of families exercising their power to change rules as they go along. The rules support family life rather than the family being there to support the rules.

We feel that adolescents find family rules difficult when they see them as being largely out of step with the rules of their own peers. (Their parents allow them to do that, why don't mine?) This is particularly so in adolescents whose parents are from a cultural background different from that in which they live – even if it is only from a different part of the country. Particularly prone to feel this are those whose families are members of ethnic minorities.

Communications often skip a generation. Adolescents may find it easier to say some things to their grandparents or listen to grandparents more than to the generation in between.

Death can be seen as a punctuation in this family life-cycle, as some members make way for others. It may seem to be stating the obvious when we say that it should not be covered up. We do so because we do not wish adolescents to be shielded from the cultural rituals to do with death, funerals and mourning. Such censorship, often imposed in the best interests of children or adolescents, makes life more difficult for them, makes it more difficult for them later to get on with the business of living. Relationships with different generations, deaths, the maintenance or separation of the relationship between their parents, and their own courtships as they develop new branches of the family, are all key issues.

Sexuality

Another obvious statement: adolescents can reproduce. This is something that parents find difficult to accept. And so do some adolescents. It seems fairly universal in developed societies that the acknowledged fun of sex for adults is something which the adults are worried that their children should discover. There are sex education classes, but few sex enjoyment classes. Most parents would probably be anxious on finding their teenagers reading *The Joy of Sex* by Alex Comfort, excellent as his book may be.

Sexual curiosity is a two-way thing. Parents are curious about the sexual life of their adolescents, even if it is only about when they first start to menstruate or ejaculate. Adolescents are curious or even incredulous about their parents' sexuality. 'Do they still do it?' is a question in many a teenager's mind. On the other hand, parental pregnancy may provide overt acknowledgement of that sexuality and may provide the opportunity for teenagers to get deeply involved in the excitement of the pregnancy in the family.

Most generations of parents seem to find their children more sophisticated than they expect; and remember how excited parents are when their child first smiles, walks or talks.

Adolescents as sexual persons start to present themselves as such to the outside world. This usually starts in play and is

23

greatly encouraged by advertising and group pressure. Parental reaction to this is very often mixed. Here is an area in which teenagers may be looking to their parents to set reasonable limits – a theme to which we refer frequently.

Dressing up has become more formalised and some of children's fashions are scaled down replicas of adult clothing.

In parents there may be a wish for their adolescents to fulfil something which they never did or are no longer able to do. This may be doing well at school, being invited to lots of parties, excelling at games. Therefore they should not be surprised to find themselves or their partners encouraging sexually provocative dress in their children.

Another sexual change may be in the sort of relationship which children have with their parents as they enter adolescence. Incest is not such a taboo subject as it used to be, but we wish to comment on what we see as a common degree of flirtatiousness between parent and teenage child. Feelings of sexual attraction are not the same as having sexual intercourse. A degree of caressing or 'accidentally' pressing part of one's body against another person are very common. For adolescents who are brought up outside families by professional carers, such behaviour may become a 'problem'. Here the adults are less prepared than are parents, already experiencing changes themselves reciprocal to the adolescent's puberty.

And of course the adolescents do indeed make friends with the opposite sex. Some of these are 'girlfriend-boyfriend' relationships. Some are not. The case of adolescents who become sexually attractive to members of their own sex is something to which we shall return later. All of these or none of these are things that may happen without being in themselves indicators of trouble to come. Adolescents vary enormously and there are many different ways of reaching adulthood.

Creativity and its Risks

The creativity of adolescents can be used as a counterpoint to the risks that are involved. Adolescents are prone to rebellion, to tribal or team loyalties. They are impressionable, the subject of peer group pressures and cults. There is the stress of school, choice of career, getting a job, friendships, other relationships. Influenced by violence, aggression, accidents, they may be involved with damage to themselves – by experimentation with drugs, alcohol, solvents, and they may even kill themselves or attempt to do so. Despite all these risks it is an enormously creative time in their lives.

Edward: computers and motor bikes

Edward was 16 and was doing well at school, where he was expected to pass several O-levels. He had two passions: computers and motor bikes. His parents encouraged the one and bought him a sophisticated home computer, but did not indulge the other, apart from a weekly subscription to a motorbike magazine.

Edward's skill at computers and designing games bore fruit when he entered a competition by a national computer games organisation. He won it and was granted copyright royalties for his game. With the first cheque of £2,500 he bought himself a motor bike and a more sophisticated computer. His parents, although very pleased with the purchase of the computer, were anxious about his purchase of the motor bike. They felt he should have saved some of the money but, more than that, they felt that the risk of riding a motor bike was one they wished he would not take. But they did not intervene because they felt it was his money and they wanted him to have control of it.

Edward started to go to a local motor-bike club. His parents were initially pleased with this because they felt that he would learn how to ride a bike safely. However this soon progressed into weekly trips to the seaside with a group of other boys on their bikes. His parents felt that the group he was going with were the unsavoury element of the club and were more interested in the excitement and the delinquent nature of motor-bike riding. His school work started to fall off. In his mock exams he got failures right across the board. His teachers were worried, asked for a meeting with his parents who also expressed their anxiety but did not feel that they knew what to do. He continued to spend most of his time at his computer or working on his bike and going out with his new-found friends.

On their way back home from a weekend trip to the seaside, the motor-cycle group encountered wet and dangerous conditions. Edward's closest friend fell off his bike and suffered severe head and leg injuries. They had all been drinking prior to the start of the journey. On his return home in a shaken and remorseful state, Edward was met by two very concerned, anxious and angry parents. To their demands that he get rid of his bike because they were unhappy with what he was doing, he replied, 'Why are you saying this to me now? It is too late. You have not said anything before, so you must think it's okay. It is my life and I shall do with it what I want.'

Edward failed all his O-levels, but his new computer game was taken on by the company and was marketed world-wide. He left school with no qualifications, a motor bike, the chance of further riches or none, and parents wondering whether they should have pruned the fruits of his creativity earlier by taking control of the first money he earned.

2

Adolescence and Society –
The Different Systems

The Family System

Seeing the family as a system is a metaphor that we have found useful and so we use it here with you.

A system is a set of objects together with the relationship between the objects and between their attributes. The objects are the components of the system; the attributes are the properties of the objects and the relationship holds it all together. When we apply this definition to a family we can see the objects as the individual family members and their attributes are their personal qualities.

Adolescents, however, are in many different systems at any one time. First, bodily and emotionally, the system of themselves.

They will have become aware, even with school athletics, how malfunction in one part of their system, say a runny nose, can affect their whole performance. They may have been aware of how, when they are feeling good about one part of their life, this affects the rest. So too in their families.

Families can be seen as being made up of several sub-systems of which the adolescent is part. They may be in the sub-system of the children taken as a whole as well as the one made up of the boys of the family or the girls. They may be in the group who are good at games, or in the sub-system of those who have not done well at school. There is the system of those who take part in household chores, or the system of those who are no good with their hands.

At school there are classes, subjects, groups, houses, sports teams. There are those who go home for dinner and there are those who have free school meals; those who are getting prepared for O-levels, those who are not; those who are grouped together who will be going on to government sponsored training schemes; the dole queue, college, university, or marriage; those who will get academic qualifications and those who will not.

They are in systems with their peers. They may be in church groups, in clubs, teams, and gangs. They may be members of one of those many sub-cultures about which parents have anxieties. Some of the current ones, although we may be out of date already, are skinheads, mods, punks, and casuals.

The Best Days of Your Life

As an adolescent, you may share the irritation that many feel at being told that your school days are the best of your life. This irritation may be intensified if it is said to you after you have been complaining about something at school. If these are the best, you may well ask, then what are the worst days going to be like? You may be irritated by our saying to you that you have got to go to school. This is because your parents have decided to take advantage of the arrangements which society has put on offer of providing the education that the law says you must be exposed to. They have chosen this rather than to try to provide it for you at home. This being so, what are you going to do with that time?

You have after all much less choice about the matter than have your teachers. They have chosen their career as schoolteachers. They can stop being schoolteachers at any time. You have not chosen your present career of being a school pupil. You may challenge it, you may defy it, you may refuse it, you may muck it up in one way or another, but you cannot stop being somebody whom society says has to go to school.

Now you may have noticed that some pupils appear to be particularly happy in their role. You may be one of them. On the other hand, you may not be. You may not be very interested in how this state of happiness is achieved. If you are not all that happy, let us see what you may be able to get from those who are. We do not mean to ask them specifically to give you something, but we suggest that by thinking about how they handle this part of their lives, you may learn something to make it easier for yourself. What is it that they are doing that is making their experience a smoother one?

They are compromising. They are accepting authority, and they have decided to enjoy as many things as they can. They are accepting what many adults call 'reality'. They have worked out what they can and cannot do well. They have worked out what they are going to have and what they are going to miss.

David: resistance and judo

David was not having a particularly good time at school. His teachers were always getting on to him and although he had some talent in quite a few subjects, his work was not going well. He was finding it difficult to give things in on time, to work to his best; and the more the teachers complained about it, the more stubborn and pigheaded he became. His work suffered accordingly. He volunteered for nothing, took part in none of the extra-curricular activities in school and seemed to get into row after row with his teachers.

The one thing that David excelled at was judo. He had represented his county at junior level and high things were hoped of him. But his performance started to suffer and, after losing a match which he had been expected to win quite easily, his coach took him to one side and said, 'Look, I don't know what is going on with you but it seems that you have started to resist a lot. Now you know that one of the secrets of this sport is that you have got to know when to push and when to give in. And you know that very often by giving way and giving in, and not resisting, you are able to get the upper hand. You seem to be resisting all the time and pushing back and your opponent is using your own strength and the way you push back in order to throw you. I think we need to work on this a bit.'

David did think about this during the next few days and, as the problem began to be ironed out in his judo, he discovered that he was not fighting and pushing back so much with his teachers. He was letting some of their comments go without retort, he was accepting more of what they were saying without complaint and he began to notice that things started to go slightly more easily for him.

School and Work

Why do parents send their children to school?
1. To educate them
2. To enhance their career prospects
3. Because the Law says so
4. To teach them about life
5. To increase their sporting skills
6. To help them meet their contemporaries and make relationships
7. To give them a life outside home
8. Because they need regular babysitters
9. Because they could not cope with them at home all the time
10. Because now they both want to go out to work.

We do not know which of these, if any, applies to you, but we do know that the higher children's intelligence and the higher they fulfil their scholastic potential, then the more likely they are to be able to end up in a job which is not as necessary to society as it is satisfying to them, a job with longer holidays, higher salary, greater social status and greater potential for borrowing money. Let us explain what we mean.

If for some reason or another we had no dustmen, the effects would soon be noticed and might constitute a danger to health. If all the barristers in the country stopped working the effects would be somewhat less tangible and more difficult to see. Given the choice of career, a dustman or a barrister, most parents would probably choose the latter for their children. Why? We are not saying that dustmen are better than barristers or vice versa. We are contrasting the two to make a point. We think that the message sometimes given implicitly to the young is, 'Work hard now, to get more rewards and satisfaction later.' Many jobs that people get as a result of doing well at school seem like leisure itself compared with the hard labour and boring experiences that others have at work. Fewer manual workers say that they enjoy their job than do non-manual workers. Is this what we mean?

It might be a useful exercise for parents to sit down and write out a list of what they want for their children from school.

When children first go to school it may give the parents their first major experience of not having first-hand knowledge of what they are doing. From now on all the information parents get is second hand. This may be the child's first experience of starting to build a relationship with adults other than parents. These are important relationships and of course children do not tell their parents all about them. They start to spend more of their active time with teachers than they do with their parents. And what parent is ever satisfied with the answer to the question, 'What did you do at school today?' Have you ever asked them not 'What did you do?' but 'Who were you with?' Talking about relationships might be more interesting.

Catherine bawled out

Catherine and her parents were going to a parents' evening at her secondary school when, on the journey there, quite suddenly and without warning, Catherine volunteered to tell her parents about something that had happened between her and the science teacher that lunchtime. He had bawled her out for her behaviour in the dining room. Her parents, amazed at this forthcomingness on behalf of their usually reticent daughter, turned off the car radio and listened intently.

'Oh, don't worry too much about it, dear' said one of them. They went into the school with some feelings of defensiveness about the daughter and anticipating that the science teacher would take this up and make an issue out of it. He did not do so. So, at the end of their interview one of them did.

A look of genuine surprise appeared on the science teacher's face. 'Oh, that,' he said, 'but that is all over and dealt with.'

Why did this happen? Maybe the teacher was also wanting to preserve that relationship which he had with Catherine. And maybe Catherine and that teacher were getting on all right after all.

How can parents cope with surrendering so much significant relationship to teachers? Prying into it closely, pestering the child and the teachers for information for what is happening is one way. But those who do this might find, as in so many other episodes in life, that the solution attempted becomes a problem in itself. Parents might find that the more they pry, the less information they get. On the other hand, ignoring it does not achieve much. One is likely to be ignored in return. It seems that the only thing for parents to do is to expose themselves as much as possible to the opportunity of obtaining information, by attending meetings, going to parents' events, buying raffle tickets, making cakes for the annual bazaar and helping at the school jumble sale. They may bump into their children's teachers, their children's peers and, dare we say it, their own children, and in that more relaxed atmosphere obtain some of the information which they need.

Homework

What about making them do their homework? We think the chances of your doing that are about the same as those of us of making you read this book, which we want you to do and to share our motivation. First, we have thought about and clarified for ourselves what we shall get out of your reading this book. Second, we have tried to put over our thoughts as clearly and simply as possible. Some things are out of our control although we tried to influence them – such as how the book is to be packaged, printed and advertised. But we also have a wish for you to extract from this book what you want. It is understandable good parenting to want your children to do their homework. Perhaps some of the things we mention above to do with your reading of this book will ring a few bells for you in thinking of some way or other that you were once helped to do things that you did not realise were in your own interests. Perhaps it will help you to think of something to do in your own family. Things that are good for your children and are also good for you are not mutually exclusive.

You can only make the setting which they may use and set the example which they may follow. We always like to express ourselves positively and, rather than saying, 'You can't go out until you've done your work', to say, 'Before you relax or before you go out, finish your homework.'

When your children complain about something that happens at school they offer their own view of the facts. If you met both of us separately we should each offer you a different view about this book because we are individuals. Of course, when your child complains to you about what has been happening at school he is not only offering a view but he is being selective about the information that is shared because he may want you to take a particular stance and show yourself to be on his side and to be sympathetic. Therefore you should not be surprised when, after your child has given you one view of a serious incident, you go to the school and hear a different one from the teachers. And things may get even more complicated when your child, in the school building, gives yet another version of the events. What the teachers are saying is only their view. You then have to develop your own view and decide how you are going to respond. Do remember that these are only views. The truth is only a concept in people's minds, particularly when they are relating an event in which they have been involved.

Michael: feelings and actions

Michael had been having a difficult time at school which had led to suspension. After much discussion with his parents the school said that they would give Michael one last chance. But they would be watching what he was doing. Michael was left in no doubt that his behaviour would be scrutinised and that he had to toe the line. His parents had a telephone call one day from the deputy head to say that Michael was being sent home immediately after being extremely rude and abusive to himself and to another teacher after a misdemeanour at school. Michael had been shouting in the classroom, and had become rude, abusive and threatening. When Michael arrived home he told his mother that they had been picking on him and that things were totally unfair. She asked him to tell her what had happened. He said, 'Just before school, just before the lesson started and we were about to sit down, Angela pulled my chair away and I fell down and shouted.

'As I fell down and was shouting, Mr Dorchester was passing and he's always got it in for me and he dragged me out of the classroom, told me I was making a nuisance of myself and hauled me off to Mr Graveney's room. I tried to explain that it was not my fault but they wouldn't listen to me. So, in the end, I got angry and started shouting and screaming at them.'

His mother said to him, 'Well, did you explain exactly what had happened?'

'Well, I tried to, but they wouldn't listen.' His mother said to him, 'Look Michael, at the moment people in school are noticing everything you do and so you have an ideal opportunity to show them all your good qualities. You may never have this chance again because pretty soon you'll be like every other kid and they won't notice you as much as they are noticing you now.'

When Michael's father came home, his mother discussed the matter with him. They went to the school the next morning with Michael, took him in, and went to see the deputy headmaster who gave them his version of what had happened. They told him what Michael had told his mother, and the deputy headmaster said that he had done some investigation and Michael's story had held out. But that was still no excuse for him to be threatening and abusive. His father said, 'But you would agree that he had reason to feel angry and unfairly treated.'

'Yes,' said the deputy headmaster, 'but that is still no excuse for him to have behaved in the way he did.'

Michael's father turned to his son and said, 'I agree with Mr Graveney. You have reason to feel unfairly treated but that is no excuse for you to be acting in that way. I do not expect that sort of behaviour from you.'

Michael said, 'I had been fooling about with Angela and winding her up before the lesson started and I suppose I was expecting her to do something back to me.'

Life after School

We all live in a social system which we call society and adolescents are part of it in its many sections. They have jobs in differing settings and have differing roles, from labourer to apprentice. They could be on youth training schemes or in the dole queue. They could go on to college or university full time. They could be in a group of young people on day release.

Adolescents are also in differing systems in their environment: the housing estate, the district, the town, the county, the country. And there are even more abstract systems involving or influencing adolescents. Some of the more established are probation departments, the police, the courts, the National Health Service, and social services.

These systems may affect the adolescent in contact with them in different ways. One way is for an adolescent to change from family living to living in an institution, the most

35

common of which are hostels or hospitals. Hospitals may be either general or psychiatric and there are community homes, youth custody and detention centres. Adolescents come to live in these places as a result of their own volition or choice, perhaps, or their parents' decision, or because society enforces it upon them. The wider system of society can say, implicitly, that it will not tolerate what an adolescent is doing and will remove him from the community at large.

Choosing a Career

We have both had careers all our lives, though we did not realise it all the time. We were both born with enormous opportunities open to us, but through a series of – we call them choices, although other people may call them circum- stances – these have been narrowed as we have aged. Each of us responded to some germs in childhood by becoming ill; each of us responded to the particular form of schooling we received by inhibiting our artistic and musical talents. We responded to the teaching of certain subjects by doing well in them, and to the teaching of others by doing badly. We narrowed our options. This process has gone on and on. Even a year ago we had a choice to meet our prospective publisher or not; then we had a choice of signing a contract or not; now we feel as if we have no choice but to finish the book.

But were they the right choices? Have our careers been the right ones for us? Those of you who are parents may wonder if your children are choosing the right career. Those of you who are adolescents may wonder if your parents are choosing the right career for themselves.

Thinking about decision-making has been central to much of our professional work. Less and less do we think that things are right or wrong, good or bad, but simply that they are happening. Hamlet said, 'There is nothing either good or bad, but thinking makes it so.' This is not to say that we do

36

not have wishes that certain things should go some ways, or should go other ways; we do have such wishes. But then how far can we go? How much of history do we wish to re-write? If we were to follow such a fantasy to its conclusion we should surely do ourselves out of existence. If that is not clear, let us explain. There is a commonly-held wish that human beings had not committed aggressive acts and that acts of aggression between countries had not taken place. We share this and yet recognise that we ourselves would not have been born had the French not invaded England in the eleventh century, or the Western European countries indulged in colonial expansionism in the seventeenth, eighteenth and nineteenth centuries. This is the case because our own backgrounds are linked in to these historical events; different branches of our family trees would not have come together if the Normans had not invaded England, nor the English colonised India. Despite not giving our approval to acts of war or colonialism, we would not be here to disapprove of them, without them.

We find this an uncomfortable paradox.

A friend once said to us,

Every time I think about how my father had to flee Nazi Germany because he was a Jew it fills me with rage. I also mourn the grandparents and family I never knew who were murdered in the concentration camps. But then I also think that if my father had not come to England he would not have married my mother and I should not be here. It sometimes causes me great pain to realise that I owe my existence to the Nazis.

So we are intrigued at the amount of energy that people put into worrying whether they are on the 'right' lines in career choices. They are the lines which they are on; they may change them voluntarily or circumstances may force them to change; they may be happy or unhappy with where their choices have led.

Some things or circumstances are preferable to others of course. Just as you prefer some characteristics of people you know to others. There are always going to be things that are liked and things that are disliked about the people one knows and about oneself.

We are not wishing to devalue the process of parental concern or of teacher advice. These seem to be just as important as what is happening in the young person. That is that, simultaneously, people of the younger generation will be facing options and changing directions in career choice, while people of the older generation will be trying to direct them, coerce them, hold them back, or be worrying about them. Both seem to be essential for the generations to live together.

Historically, societies have categorised their members. From the Hindu caste system to the British notion of class. It is simple to divide people into different classes. You may feel that this is only relevant to sociologists. But different statistical predictions can be made about the progress or careers of members of those classes. Some sociologists have pointed out that often working-class children who get degrees at university go on to become teachers for the length of their earning careers. They thus 'choose' to 'remain' at school and to continue in that pattern of behaviour which was so highly valued, namely 'doing well at school'.

Schoolteaching has other implications which interest us. Until fairly recently pupils on leaving school could go on to take unskilled jobs and earn more than teachers themselves. Of people with degrees, teachers must be among the most lowly paid, with the possible exception of the clergy. Why is this? It is almost as if they are seen by society as child-minders and no more. A derogatory view? Well, how did the profession start?

Parents could not cope with bringing up their children, looking after them, or giving them information about what was available in society – parents could not manage to give them all this in the manner they wished. Additionally, parents nowadays wish to have the satisfaction of careers for themselves and cannot arrange both without employing minders for their children. Current legislation about education supports our view. The law does not say that children must be educated; nor does it say that children must go to school. It simply says that they must be exposed to education. Now, rather than organise this for themselves, most parents send their children to schools where it is done for them.

It is, of course, well known that children – like adults – if left to themselves get up to mischief. *Lord of the Flies* by William Golding provides the most graphic example of this. To control anxiety about the sort of mischief that children will get up to, teachers are very useful. In fact they are about the best thing there is.

The exception to our view about teachers lies in the Jewish tradition where the rabbi is held in high esteem.

The Law

All families have an experience of the law. We think they may be particularly likely to have this during the adolescence of the younger generation because adolescents do a number of things which are 'risky'. Additionally, there are many prohibitive laws which have boundaries to do with the age of adolescence – when you can buy alcohol, have sex, drive motor-cycles or cars. The law applies to all and adults who have the vote have a say in how it is made.

The police are used to enforce the law but are separate from the law. We think it is important for us to keep this distinction in our minds. We recognise that we are open to criticism for holding too simplistic a view, but we ask people to bear with us because we do find this way of seeing things as useful in looking at the process of adolescents and families. We hope that this may become apparent.

If families have not yet had the experience of the law

directly, then we recommend that they anticipate it and expect the unexpected.

We should like to ask a question of all parents reading this book – what do you think you would feel if you learned that your son or daughter had been breaking the law? And what do you think you would feel if the action which was breaking the law was (a) breaking the speed limit, (b) burglary, (c) drinking alcohol in licensed premises when under age, (d) taking part in secondary picketting, or (e) smuggling a member of an oppressed minority from a country which forbade it. We think that you would have different responses. If the offence was hitting a policeman when the adolescent was being arrested for burglary, we think you may respond differently than you would if this act was committed when the adolescent was being constrained during a political demonstration.

Families encourage attitudes about the law – that they are just, unjust or irrelevant. Families have values about the law – that it is important to obey it or that it is important not to be caught disobeying it.

Function of the Law

What are laws? They are there and so they have a function. We see laws as guidelines from society about expected behaviour. We see the conviction and punishment of some people who break the law as drawing the attention of everybody else to the guidelines.

There is a difference between the law and the norm of society. There are rules and *rules*.

In families there are rules which are explicit and rules which are implicit. For example, 'Nobody leaves the table until everybody finishes the meal.' This has been said by the parents, and children have been taught so to behave. On the other hand, that nobody sits in Dad's armchair or that nobody contradicts grandmother, are unspoken implicit rules which none the less are very powerful. Difficulties in families often occur when the implicit rules contradict the explicit rules. 'Don't do what I do. Do what I say.'

Sometimes the norms of society, the laws of the land and the rules of a particular institution, coincide. Sometimes they do not. Both of us have worked in institutions where, if we were to have had sexual intercourse with a 16-year-old, we should have lost our jobs. If the 16-year-old had been a girl, then our act in itself would not have been illegal but we should have broken a very powerful norm or rule of society. If the 16-year-old had been a boy, then we should have broken not only the norm but also a law.

Robert: speeding and burglary

Robert's parents, Ruth and Simon, had been easy-going with him as had most of their friends been with their own children. They had their own rules and sometimes they would reprimand Robert for his transgressions, but sometimes they would not. He had a lot of freedom and was often out fairly late at night but remained civil enough to his parents for them to feel reasonably content.

Simon had been caught for speeding at the beginning of the year, appeared in court, made an apologetic statement and was promptly fined. He described it as just one of those things and was observed by Robert to drive at about the same speed as before but with a much more careful eye on the mirror.

Ruth was horrified one day when two uniformed policemen appeared at the door to interview Robert, who had been accused of burglary. It all came out. He had indeed burgled a house with two other boys on the previous Saturday when Ruth and Simon thought he was at a party.

As a result of the shock the three of them came together but hardly knew what to say to each other. Robert certainly appeared crestfallen and ashamed. Ruth and Simon were caught up in feeling angry with their son for breaking the law and also wondering how they could arrange matters so that he got off with the lightest possible penalty. Simon said to Ruth that it was just like Robert to have been caught the first time he did anything. They took some consolation from the fact that it was apparently the first time that he had done something so wrong.

All of us break the law and continue to do so. Sunday trading is a current example. If the law-breaking becomes more than a certain degree, then there is pressure not to enforce the law but to change it, as with discussion about motorway speed limits in the middle 1980s.

Leisure

Are you reading this for pleasure or because you have to?

A traveller came upon a man dozing under a tree by a river. The traveller asked: 'What are you doing?'

MAN: 'I am sitting under this tree.'
TRAVELLER: 'Haven't you anything better to do?'
MAN: 'Like what?'
TRAVELLER: 'Well, you could get a job and if you worked hard you would do well and earn some money.'
MAN: 'And then what?'
TRAVELLER: 'Well, after enough time you would be able to get a better home and provide more things for your family.'
MAN: 'And then what?'
TRAVELLER: 'Well, then you would have the time and the money to do the things that you really wanted to do.

'What do you really like to do best of all?'
MAN: 'Sitting under a tree, dozing, by this river.'

Leisure is to be Taken Seriously

Adolescents work hard at their leisure. So do some adults, even watching TV.

Leisure is an important part of our lives. It is where many

relationships are formed and maintained, where much emotional exploration or intellectual stimulation takes place. In leisure people may maintain their bodies to prevent coronaries. It is something which should, in our view, be taken very seriously.

Adolescents are often given double messages. On the one hand they should work hard and enjoy the satisfaction of that. On the other hand adults speak of the relief of the weekend.

The TV programme 'Why don't you get out of your chair and do something less boring' has been running for years. We believe that it is not difficult to encourage people to get out of their chairs and do something other than watching television; to change people from being passive participants to active ones. We feel this is particularly so with adolescents. If, given the choice of watching television or going swimming or joining in a fair, we think they are more likely to choose to go out. If choices are not arranged for them, they may arrange their own choices, about some of which parents may feel anxious or disapprove: such as delinquency, glue-sniffing, having sex.

We think television is an influence because it is allowed to be an influence. We have no doubt of the conclusions from many researches that television violence influences young viewers to be more violent. This is not surprising for, after all, we do accept that television advertisements influence people to buy what is advertised. Video nasties therefore can be a problem, simply because parents use video as a cheap form of babysitting. Again, we do emphasise that we are not trying to take sides in this issue or to say that we disapprove of parents buying videos for their families, or to say that it is 'easy' to provide alternatives. Simply, we are saying that this is something which is happening. This is part of what is going on today between the generations.

Creative Censorship

We regret that censorship is seen as a negative thing. We find it difficult to discuss the research evidence about television violence without emotive reactions from colleagues about censorship and freedom. In fact we see censorship going on all the time. To switch on Channel A is to censor Channel B.

In one of the institutions in which we have worked the film *Scum*, which portrayed life in youth custody, was being shown on television. The adolescents were not allowed to watch this by the staff. The adolescents said that this decision was not fair. If they were at home they would be allowed to watch it. This was accepted by the staff: 'Yes, we agree that if you were at home or anywhere else you very probably would be allowed to watch this film, but we have decided that we feel too anxious about you watching a film like this.' The adolescents accepted the decision without much fuss.

Institutions and Parental Responsibility

Nearly all children go to school to be exposed to education according to the law.

Because the law is so unclear, we again take a simple view, which is that when someone is under the age of 16 their parents, or whoever has parental authority, must decide where they live and must arrange for medical treatment. Therefore, if you as parents are told that your daughter or son should go into hospital or to a boarding school, to an assessment centre or to a children's home, the decision is yours, unless a court has decided that it should be somebody else's decision.

Daphne: going home again

Daphne was a mentally handicapped girl living in an institution for which she had become too old. Another institution was asked to take her and sent some of their staff to discuss it. One of the first things the visitors asked was what Daphne's parents wanted.

They were told that Daphne's parents were inadequate – the mother was described as mentally ill land the father as simple and unemployed. The visitors said they would refuse to consider the case further unless they met the parents as well as Daphne. They were told that the parents would probably not come because they had rarely visited.

A meeting with the parents did take place, however, and they did indeed 'look' inadequate. When they were questioned about not having visited their daughter, the parents said they had been told by their own psychiatrist not to visit because of the mother's condition.

Asked what they themselves wanted, both parents said that they wished to have Daphne home, and Daphne smiled assent. The institution's social worker protested saying that their housing was too inadequate to accommodate Daphne.

The visitors asked if the social worker was so anxious about Daphne's parents' accommodation that she would apply to a magistrate for a Place of Safety Order to remove the child? Which parenting environment gave the social worker most anxiety – home with her chronically mentally-ill mother and out-of-work father who wanted her, a local authority children's home, or a mental handicap hospital? The social worker thought that they were all much of a muchness as far as her anxiety was concerned, but if the parents did take Daphne home then she would offer them her support.

The parents were reminded by the visitors that Daphne could go home only if they, the parents, decided. Because they held parental authority they were the ones who had to make the decision. If the staff from the social services department disagreed with them, they had to work out a legal way to stop them. The parents made the decision to have their daughter home, and Daphne smiled again.

3

Strategies for Coping and Change

Life at Home: Planning v. Happening

On any number of occasions in our own lives we have achieved things that in the past we would have thought possible only by the waving of a magic wand. When we were adolescents we would not have predicted that we could have, nor dreamed that we would ever want, our present jobs. Such jobs were not even in our own minds until we were about 30. Sometimes we seem to have planned most carefully the course of events and feel pleased by the achievement. Sometimes it seems as if it just 'happened' and we feel lucky. Which is the right feeling to have? A lot of the time we find it difficult to believe that we are writing this book and we wonder how long it will take us to accept or really believe that it has been published. We sometimes wonder how we have achieved all this and by what criteria we measure it. As for the sense of achievement – how do we grade ours compared with that experienced by, say, the novelist Christie Brown, who typed using his toe, or our own feelings when we built our first sandcastle?

We both had grandmothers who told us not to cross our bridges until we came to them, but both of us, when we start a journey, try to find out where we might need a bridge. Some things we can plan at the start and some we leave until later. Others just seem to happen.

John and Gwen Arkwright and hard work

John Arkwright worked as a bus conductor and before Matthew was born Gwen had worked as a secretary in an office. They had looked forward to Matthew's starting school because this meant that Gwen could go back to work to supplement the family income. A bonus that they then appreciated greatly was that Matthew enjoyed school from the start and did well. As Matthew's school career progressed, Gwen and John would occasionally have some contact with the school at parents' evenings and other events. By the time he had started secondary school his parents' interest in his work, although remaining, became less specific as his achievements outstripped their own capability of understanding.

Matthew successfully sat several O-levels and went on to do his A-levels. He was hoping for a career at university. Shortly before Matthew was to take his A-levels, John was made redundant because the local council had decided to privatise the bus service and did not need as many bus conductors. Matthew felt indignant at what had happened to his father because, alongside his academic achievements, he had developed an interest in politics – and even thought of it as a possible future career. His politics were left wing and his passionate views were even more forcefully expressed now that he felt he had a very personal cause to champion. The unemployment debate had a special significance.

After A-levels Matthew went on to university to read politics and philosophy. He was soon involved in university life and when asked about his family, he was proud to say that his father was unemployed – a victim of the policies of right-wing government. When asked what his father used to do Matthew appeared less proud and forthcoming; he usually mumbled something about involvement in transport.

Matthew got his first-class degree and his parents were very proud of him at the graduation ceremony. He introduced them to his tutors and fellow students, still taking pride in introducing his father as unemployed. Six months after graduation Matthew, for all his trying, was still not able to get a job. Doors through which he was interested in going, such as the Civil Service, or the trade union movement, were not being opened for him. He tried his hand at writing, because his tutors had said he had talent; but he could find no one to buy his work.

On a visit home at Christmas, Matthew said to John, 'Dad, I just don't know how you manage to be unemployed.' John replied, 'Son, you just have to work at it.'

We decided to write this book because many parents had spoken to us about difficulties they had with their teenage children and many teenage children had spoken to us about the difficulties they had with their parents. In all our conversations with them, one often-repeated phrase was 'the harder I tried, the worse the problem got'. On the occasions when things had got better it was usually when the people involved had started to do things in a different way; when they had thought of doing something differently; when a friend or relative or somebody outside the immediate family had suggested something different; when they had got the idea from a film they had seen, or a television programme, or a book, or a conversation overheard in a bus, or sheer inspiration.

Very often, in the chronic problems in people's minds, they feel that they have tried everything that they can think of, but closer examination often shows that they have been trying to do the same thing in different ways. Very soon they start a self-perpetuating cycle and any attempted solution becomes the problem:

> The more you keep your room untidy as a response to your mother's nagging, the more she nags.
> The more you nag your son about his untidy room, the untidier it gets.

Adults and teenage children easily get caught up in the cycle of nagging and getting nagged. They find themselves caught: one side nagging the other because they do not listen and the other not listening because they are nagged. The more the nagging – an attempted solution to the not listening – the more the children do not listen; and the more they do not listen – an attempted solution to the nagging – the more the parents nag. Both attempted solutions have become a problem.

'Very well,' you may say to us, 'but we have tried everything else. It just is very hard to get them to listen (or to stop nagging).' Yes you may very well be right. We are not offering an easy or magic solution to any problem; we are simply suggesting that looking in a different direction may open things up.

Very often, for things to change for the better, people have to act or think differently. It is almost like seeing things through a different pair of eyes. Very often, things that seem the most crazy, unusual, or hard to bear, may be just the sort of thing that might bring a change. Because the chances are that it will not be 'more of the same'.

We think that this is such an important point that we are going to go over it yet again, from one of the points of view – that of the adults. Your children are not listening to you and so you nag them. Now you know that in order to get somebody to listen to you, you must first have their attention. There are many ways of doing this. When you find that your particular way of trying to get your children's attention is not working, try something different. For example, you tell your child to be in by 11 p.m. She does not come in until 1 a.m. You tell her off about it. She obviously does not listen to you because she keeps on doing it. Apparently the more you start acting the authoritarian parent the less notice is taken of you. In other cases, being the authoritarian parent and laying the law down in a heavy way may work very well, and if this works with your child then please continue it.

If being the heavy authoritarian parent is not working, however, then you may like to think of other ways to get your child's attention. One variant to 'You must come in at 11 o'clock or else' might be 'I should like you to come in at 11 o'clock but I don't expect you to take much notice of me. So goodbye.' We are pretty sure that the latter statement after a long run of the former is more likely to grab children's attention and get them to start listening to you. We hope that any difference in the relationship may help both of you to get what you want. Do remember that with even that little example there are so many different ways of saying the words. If you say it in your usual tone of voice for that sort of statement it then becomes what we have called 'doing the same things differently'.

Everybody has a particular way of seeing things, including what they see as a problem. People talk about their 'problem' and its effect on their lives rather than doing something different. They seem to prefer it that way, but we think that it is only an appearance. We think that by doing something different, no matter how small, at least a different view is obtained of the problem. With this different way of seeing it the talking may take on a different quality, particularly if it is about changes.

When examining the problem you have with your children, or with your parents, we suggest you think of three questions; they might bring up interesting answers.
1. What is the problem?
2. How is it a problem to you?
3. What are you trying to do about it?

Problem Parents

Even the best organised who appear very self-sufficient and independent have parents on whom they depended. Most adolescents have parents who are alive and active during their adolescence, dead but never completely forgotten, or somewhere in between. It is often in our teenage years that suspicions about parents having faults become certainties. Their feet of clay are all too clear.

Those of you who are parents but who are reading this

section, which is really designed for teenagers, may care to ask yourselves how much of what we are saying is still relevant to you as parents. We all go on having a bit of the teenager in us.

In teenage, boys and girls become more embarrassed by the presence of parents, by meeting them in the street and their expectation to be introduced to friends. What do you do with them at parties? Worst of all may be when they come to school. The most caring, concerned parents who come to support their adolescent children or to question their teachers have no idea how embarrassing this may be for the adolescents themselves.

Part of the process of separation is starting to detach oneself from, and not identifying with, parents. A usual experience for teenagers is to wonder if they may have been adopted because 'It is difficult to see how parents like them can possibly have produced someone like me.'

An exercise which might be of interest is to ask your friends to write down some of your qualities and some of your parents' qualities and to see how many similarities there may be. A further exercise is to work towards a definition of perfect parents: write a list of properties that perfect parents would have. Ask yourself if you know any and also ask your friends how your parents measure up to this list.

A group exercise can be for adolescents to describe their parents as objectively as they can and to write this on paper or on the computer. The descriptions are shuffled in a hat and picked out. The task then is to try to identify which parents are which.

Perfection does not exist. It is only a standard made by people by which they measure others. The differences, that is the imperfections, are the reality. The parents you have are the best you have got. If you are having difficulties with them, then all you have to learn is how to deal with them.

Paradoxically, it really would be impossible for you if your parents were perfect. Imagine what it would be like to live with people who did the right thing every time. Assumed perfection as a human trait is the biggest imperfection.

In talking to adolescents we have found that areas which particularly concern them about their parents are:

1. Adolescents feel that parents continue to treat them as if they were younger than they are. In their presence, the adolescents feel continually under pressure to be different or to meet a certain standard or to be compared with their friends. They are nagged and embarrassed by this.
2. Parents fail to recognise sufficiently the separateness of their adolescent children. That they have their own friends and want to be with them and want to be with their friends' families.
3. Secrecy. Parents want to know everything. It is not that the teenager may have anything to hide but the teenager resents the feeling that everything must be known and shared.

Teasing

Parents tease their children and they laugh about things you adolescents consider very serious, like having a row with your girlfriend or not getting your hair style right. Why do they do it?

They enjoy it and it gives them a sense of power. You could try being a bit more secretive but that is not likely to help much. You can try teasing them back but they are likely to be better at it than you. Your parents have probably learned that to survive they have had to learn not to take everything too seriously and may be trying to teach you that. Try to appreciate that at least, even if the teasing itself probably feels uncaring and insensitive.

Secrets and Privacy

We are interested in the difference between secrets and privacy. In writing this book we have shared some of our thoughts with you, some we have not. We have shared some aspects of ourselves, but some we have kept to ourselves. If the things we have kept to ourselves are simply what would generally be considered to be aspects of our private lives, such as what our sex lives are like, what our marriages are like, how much we feel loved and respected or hated by those close to us, how much money we earn, then we are sure that you will consider the reasons for not sharing this sort of information to be legitimate as it is our private business. We agree. We do not think that withholding this sort of information from you affects our relationship with you. On the other hand, if some of the information we held from you was that either of us had been banned from our work because we had been found guilty of abusing the trust that young people had in us, we think you would feel very differently and it would affect our relationship.

So our definition of a secret is information that is withheld because of a fear that it would affect one's relationship with another. But the effect on the relationship need not be an adverse one. We believe that there are benevolent secrets. Not to tell a child what she is getting for Christmas is to maintain a feeling of excitement and the experience of surprise on opening the parcel. Similarly, the intention of parents not to tell their children the intricacies of reproduction may be to preserve what they consider a sense of innocence in children. Also, telling children explicitly or implicitly that everything will be all right is to protect them from the 'secret' that life is not like that.

This country even has an Official Secrets Act.

So if secrets are so much a part of everyday life and everybody realises early on in existence that they have the power to manufacture or maintain them, why do parents make such a meal out of them? But they do.

Parents keep secrets for the best of motives. Perhaps sometimes their children also have good motives for having secrets. How do you know when your child or your parent is keeping a secret from you? Do they look furtive; do you feel suspicious; do they start acting very differently, or what?

Three secrets

JANE

Jane's parents were shocked to find glue and a plastic bag in her bedroom and, of course, confronted her with this. It had been a secret. Her friend Jennifer had tried glue-sniffing, had been very sick and Jane had taken the stuff from her. Not knowing what to do with it, but fearing her parents would be very anxious if they knew, she hid it. It was a secret.

ALISON

Alison got back in time from the party and her parents were not anxious about her. They would have been had they known that she had not come home with her friends but had accepted a lift from an older man who was leaving at the same time. Nothing happened in the car, but because Alison felt that the knowledge of this would worry her parents unduly, and might lead them to consider limiting her freedom, she decided to keep it a secret.

HENRY

Henry was due to take his university finals. Although a brilliant scholar he had always had difficulty with his examinations. In his usual weekly telephone call home, he was a bit surprised to learn that his dad was out but thought no more about it. The following week, an hour or so before his usual time to telephone home, he was surprised that his mother rang him first. 'Just for a chat', she said, 'and Uncle Bill is here. Dad's out testing the car.'

After his exams, Henry learned that his father had been in hospital for those two weeks, dangerously ill. They had not told him because they did not want to worry him before his exams.

Henry's parents had put a value on his passing his exams higher than the value they put on his seeing his father before his father died, should his father have been going to die.

We wondered a great deal in our work and in our writing if such values could ever be measured against each other. On what scale, upon which criteria, with which measurement, could parents compare Henry's passing of exams with his seeing his father before his death, or knowing and worrying about an illness which may or may not have been terminal? In ten years' time, looking back on university life, would Henry be more pleased if he passed his exams although his father had died, or if he had known about his father's death, visited him and failed his exams? Of course it can never be known if he would have failed or passed the exams if he also had had the worry about his father.

We have decided in our professional lives that it is best not to have secrets in our work and to encourage families, whose corporate distress is such that they consult us, at least to work on their secrets.

If we keep from Dan that Uncle Maurice has just killed himself, we are not just keeping information about Uncle Maurice, we are also keeping from Dan information about himself, because Dan is now a different person: he is some-body who had an uncle who killed himself.

What would you do if, in the middle of Melanie's final O-level examination, you learned that her mother had just died? Would you take her out of the exam and tell her there and then or would you wait until she had finished? What is best?

Andrew's adoption researches

Arthur and Jenny had adopted a baby boy (Andrew) and made no secret of this. They were one of the most open couples that we had come across. They introduced the information about adoption very early on in children's stories. Unlike some couples who feel that the main reason that information about adoption should be shared early is because they wish to avoid their child's finding out by himself, Arthur and Jenny felt that their son had a right to know this information and that was what was best for him. They wished to share their mutual joy. Arthur often told his son 'The information is all in the desk upstairs. I don't want to push it on you. But if you ever want to know something, you come and we'll have a look through it and see what we can find.'

They were not surprised that he asked so little, because they felt that the whole matter had been dealt with so openly.

Many years later, a friend working at the Town Hall surprised them by telling them that Andrew had been making enquiries of his own about his genealogy. He had contacted the social worker responsible who had done some searching for him and found out details of his adoption.

Even though they were at first angry with their friend for betraying Andrew's own confidential enquiry and acknowledging that he was exercising his right to trace his natural parents, Arthur and Jenny were shattered by the news. They had a family conference and beseeched their adopted son to tell them where they had gone wrong. He reassured them that they had not gone wrong at all. He simply wanted to find out for himself. 'But why, in heaven's name, why, did you not ask us? We have it all in this drawer and you could have seen it.'

'Ah' said Andrew, 'but I wanted you to go on having a secret from me. I wanted you to feel that you really did know something about me which I did not know, because it made me feel closer.'

Untidiness

Untidiness is in the eyes of the beholder. The wife of one of us said, 'Before I started living with you I thought I was untidy.'

What is it about your over-tidy houseproud parents that gets you going? Let us look at what parents have to do. Parents are managers. They have to decide what clothes to buy for their children and to make decisions about measuring, budgeting, assessing, calculating. They have to decide how much food to cook for supper, how many blankets to put on the bed, what quality wallpaper and carpet to buy, how much money to allocate to holidays, to decorations, to clothing, to essential repairs of the house, to leisure and to pocket money. They have to take decisions about elementary precautions such as safety in the house, and where matches, poisonous and inflammable articles are stored. For a family to have got to the stage of having adolescent children at all, the parents must have managed this pretty well. The way the parents have led the family offers the adolescents a model.

How is the adolescent to know the right amount of food to eat without trying to eat too much? How is the adolescent to decide standards of orderliness, management and planning without experimenting around those standards set by the parents? How can we have any order in our lives without measuring it against some chaos? How can we have identity without boundaries and difference?

Martin and untidiness

Martin's room was always in a mess and his chaos seemed to infiltrate every part of the house. There were bits of his bicycle, fishing tackle, his school books and various games, records, all sorts of paraphernalia that teenagers have around them, scattered around the house. All his mother's nagging and tidying up and his father's shouting at him seemed to have no effect. Owen and Sally Webster were not particularly houseproud people, but they liked a certain amount of order around them. Owen had worked hard at building up the house and Sally had a part-time job as a school dinner lady. Martin, at 16, had become fairly used to a good material standard of living and seemed to take a lot of things for granted.

Owen and Sally were sitting in the living-room one evening, while Martin was out at his youth club, and were talking about their untidy son and what to do about it. 'I'm really at my wits' end about it' said Sally, 'because he is a decent enough lad but I find that I am not talking to him about anything else. I just keep rowing with him about his room, and when you come back from work I keep telling you about it and the first thing you say is to tell him off rather than talking to him about the other things I know you like talking to him about. It seems to be putting a barrier between us and I don't know what we can do.'

Owen replied, 'Well I was talking to Fred at work and he said, "Why don't you give him a taste of his own medicine?"'

'Well, what does that mean?' asked Sally.

'Why don't we start becoming untidy and leaving stuff lying around the place and messing up things and let him see what it is like. We can go into his room and mess it up, and we can leave things around, not do the washing-up and you need not do the washing. Just relax; we won't say anything about it, we shall just start doing these things.'

Over the course of the next few days, the tidiness in the Webster household took a dive. Sally did stop doing the washing and all the washing-up after meals. Pans remained dirty, there were fish-and-chip papers scattered all over the place. At first Martin did not say very much but just kept on using clean clothes and clean plates as they were available.

After the first week, on going to his room and finding no clean clothes to wear, he went to his mother and said, 'Hey Mum, there are no clean clothes for me to wear.'

'Oh, aren't there?' said his mother. 'I wonder what is on television now?' And she put the television set on and started to watch her favourite soap opera.

Martin was rather amused at this and went to his room and found some socks on the floor and washed them for school the next morning. His room still remained in a mess but the real dramatic change in his own tidiness and cleaning up took place when he returned from his youth club one evening to find his father dismantling the broken washing machine in Martin's bedroom. 'What are you doing, Dad?' he asked.

Owen replied, 'I've got no other place to do this, Martin. There is stuff all over the place and your bedroom floor seems to be the only place I can do this. I wouldn't worry about it; it'll only take me two or three weeks to fix it – until I get the spare parts – so I'll just leave the washing machine and its bits here until I've sorted it out.'

'Come on, Dad, you can't do that. The place is in an entire mess. We can't live like this.'

Owen said nothing and went on fixing the washing machine, and within a few weeks Martin had started washing-up after himself, washing some of his clothes and keeping his room to a different standard. Untidiness was no longer dominating family life as it used to.

Fixing Goals

Whatever the problem that is being faced, swimming a length, passing an examination or being jilted by a lover, it is all too easy to get it out of perspective. We have found many people have been helped by taking a different view of their problem, often as if it were someone else's view. This then makes it easier for them to decide on a goal for themselves. Remember how good you are at thinking of solutions for other people's problems.

The goal in adolescence may be clear enough: to get through it. The goal in particular moments of adolescence or in the handling of particular themes in the relationships involved, may be much less clear.

We recommend that any adolescent who feels that he or she has a problem with parents, relatives, friends or anything should sit down, reflect and decide on a goal. This goal should be something that is realistically achievable, rather than idealistic. Achieving the goal should be the signal that the problem is on its way to being managed. We advise caution against setting a goal which has as its aim the end of the problem. That is just too much. If there is a choice of two or three achievable aims, we recommend taking the easiest of these. The others can come later.

If the goal is defined, then it is possible to look at strategies. A strategy is a planned course of action to achieve, with the least effort, the least change with which one will be satisfied – just enough to feel on one's way, to feel, for example, that your parents are just that bit more off your back. This may mean sacrifice or surrender of principle to a degree. This may mean showing some courtesy and paying some attention to tidiness and homework.

And simply sharing one's experience with one's own age group often produces remarkable similarity of experience, and support.

We are writing here about the way most people are. Of course there are parents who get drunk, neglectful, violent, demanding, deviant, immoral, unfair; who handle their marriages, or divorces, or mistresses, or lovers clumsily and who trample others, often their children, underfoot. What do you do if you are brought up and caught up with the likes of such? What do you do, that is, without going to the police or social services department for the help which is yours by right of statute?

We think that there are ways of making things which seem intolerable a bit better. And here are some.

The first is to do with space: keeping out of the way. This can be done physically, by leaving the house or by avoiding nearness to the parent at the times known to be problematic. It is also possible to get away by indulging one's fancy in a good book.

Moments of acute provocation can sometimes be helped by the apparently very simple manoeuvre of concentrating on one's breathing, of lengthening the breath, taking note of it and its effect on the body. Such a simple introspective exercise we have often found helpful in situations which otherwise we should have found very provocative. It is called 'taking a deep breath and counting to ten'.

Another very good way of coping, which is much maligned, is crying. This not only offers an enormous relief of feelings for the one that cries but has profound influence upon others around. We very much regret that sexual discrimination in our upbringing which, by the rule that boys did not cry, rendered us somewhat handicapped in this skill.

Humour can be used, if used with great care. As a young child you were probably capable of turning maternal wrath into laughter; but, as words get more and more your main means of communication, you may have lost this ability. It may be worth experimenting with this again because it is a useful life skill – even if it does not work with your family problems.

We think that concentrating on positives is a good idea. You might find it difficult to see any positive things in your life but, believe us, there are. Find out what you are good at and if this can be coupled with an activity which brings out your skills, which you also enjoy, it is a useful way of creating space for yourself.

The other thing that we forget so much when we are involved in conflict or problem, is the context of time. Everything is temporary and will end. At the simplest level we may forget the family's regular time for moments of stress. For many families it is Sunday morning. A diary or chart may be quite useful.

In the longer term we think it is important to remember that adolescence is a temporary phase and that the relationship between adolescent and parents lasts only a few years.

Thomas, Paula and their father's low times

Thomas and Paula got on with their parents more or less as well as could be expected in adolescence and used to have the occasional massive row with their father, who was a successful salesman in a high-pressure industry. Certainly the family's material standards were high: they lived in a good house, a pleasant neighbourhood, had most of the usual material possessions that one could want, had good holidays. From time to time they found their father, normally quite a fair, reasonable, just man, to be totally irrational. He would swear, shout and be particularly tetchy and bad tempered. Their mother used to say to them, 'Just keep out of your father's way.' They found it difficult to do so.

At the age of 16, Thomas discovered that these times when his father was particularly difficult coincided with times when

61

he was due to land a big order. Thomas deduced that the tension was building up in his father to such an extent that it was spilling over at home. He talked about this to his sister, who was two years younger, and they decided that they would try to find out when their father was due to land a big order. At those times they would just keep out of his way. Fortunately both of them had a keen interest in games and simply increased their practice sessions at the times of their father's stress. As their father approved heartily of their sporting prowess, this was a solution which was agreeable to all.

Gareth and his nagging mother

Gareth was always being nagged about the tidiness of his room. He decided to have a tidy project and that he would be prepared to tidy his room eleven times in any year. With his computer he worked out eleven random dates. When the first of these came he tidied his room beautifully – that is, he tidied so that it looked good. He then arranged for his mother to see it. This worked out fairly easily the first time, but on the third date he had to create 'an accident' to get her to come into his room: he said that he had spilt something on his carpet and it was terrible. His mother rushed in but could hardly find the spot which he showed. She then noticed the rest of the room and expressed a great admiration for how he was keeping it.

Linda and her telephone calls

Linda knew that her parents were worried about what she was getting up to: staying out late at night and sometimes staying with her friends. She knew from bitter experience that her parents would sometimes go over the top about this, call the police or ring her friends at embarrassing times. Quite by accident she discovered that ringing her parents when she was having one of her evenings out, and asking in a very cheering voice 'How are you' and 'What are you doing this evening?' made them feel good. Even in his later years Linda's father was never able to decide whether she did this strategically or because she really felt concerned, and he was certainly never able to get round to asking her. Of course if he had asked her he would never have known whether her answer was truthful or not. But he was sure that it made him feel better.

Whatever it is that you do, please try to remember to have a measurable and positive goal. It is really not much good deciding to use, say, a tactic to do with space unless it is measured. For how many minutes in the day do you have to be alone and in your own space to make you feel that you have got somewhere or turned a corner with your problem? If you are going to use one of the other strategies, for how many minutes in the day would you have to be replacing the current thoughts or experiences to do with your awful parents, with ones that give you more pleasure, for you to feel that you are getting somewhere?

If your problem is being sworn at by your parents, then do not think of what reduction in the amount of swearing would be a satisfactory goal for you, for that is a negative change. Try to find a positive one. Your goal might be as simple as that you and your parents spend half an hour a week, awake, in the same building, even in silence; or, that once during the week your parents say 'Thank you' to you.

How to Cope with Nagging Parents

If you are fed up with your parents nagging you about the state of your room, we suggest you try to work out the least bit of change that has to take place that will keep them quiet. Only one of the ways of finding this out is by asking them. There are other ways. We call one way experimenting. Tidy up a little bit and, if they still nag, tidy up a little bit more until you reach a point when they don't nag you any more. You probably find that the room is still individually yours and you have stopped your parents talking to you about it. Remember, if you want to keep your privacy, then you have got to stop them from going into your room. If the room is in such a state that they want to talk about it all the time then you are not doing very well at keeping them out. Take a note of the particular times of the week when your parents nag you most about your room and you can make a special effort to keep it tidy on those occasions. We do not offer you advice or suggestions from the point of view of 'getting one over' on your parents, but note that in family life there are more interesting ways to spend time than nagging and arguing about the state of rooms. Your parents may have particular difficulties and pressures, one of which may be exacerbated by the state of your room. If you can be helpful in getting them to stop nagging about your room then you are acting as a dutiful child in enabling both yourself and them to spend time on things which may be mutually beneficial and more productive.

We hope that any parents reading this section will remember what we have said earlier about attempted solutions (see p. 48).

Our view is that parents are in charge of their teenage children, but that there are different ways of being in charge. One of the ways is to let those in your charge help you.

Doug's agreement

Doug hated his mother's coming into his room. On the other hand he did not like using the vacuum cleaner but found that it was absolutely necessary if he was not to feel quite wheezy. His hobby was computers and he knew that dust might interfere with his equipment. He and his mother eventually worked out a compromise.

They made an agreement about what she was responsible for in his room and what he was responsible for. They wrote it all down and signed it and got his father to sign it as a witness. It started almost as a game. He kept this piece of paper and found it helpful when he or his mother wanted to remind the other when the agreement had been broken. They agreed that if Doug broke the agreement he would be 'sentenced' to reading one of his mother's women's magazines, which he abhorred; if she broke the agreement, she would have to read one of his computer magazines, which she could not understand. Neither could think of a worse penalty for the other.

The Treat Home like a Hotel

Parents often complain that their teenage children treat the home like a hotel. They flit in and out at mealtimes, come in late, go to bed, go to sleep, use all the amenities of the house, eat the food, get warmth from the heating, watch the television, and seem to make little contribution to its upkeep. They seem not to realise that their parents by choosing their home, arranging its purchase or rental, furnishing it, may have a bigger commitment and feelings about it than their children. At the end of a stay in a hotel there is a bill to pay. Adolescents may not only treat home like a hotel but one which has free rooms on offer. They may even expect room service. In a television programme when some adolescents were talking about things to put on their hair to style it in different fashions, a girl of 15 said of a particular method, 'All you need is sugar and water, and because you get them out of the kitchen, they cost nothing.'

Although parents will recognise the irony of the girl's statement, as if sugar magically appeared on the kitchen shelves, the teenagers in the programme acted as if such magic really did occur.

Milton Erickson, an American psychiatrist, once said 'Of course children should play their part in housework, because it is their contribution to the home.' We add that, of course, it is their home but it is your house or flat.

Our Home is not our Home any More

Adolescents can be awful. They can show no gratitude. All their remarks about the food you prepare for them can be complaints. They can do nothing but complain. You may fear to have any conversation with them lest complaints, ingratitude, insolence erupt immediately.

They may feel somewhat the same. They may feel that the only time you talk to them is to complain to them or to nag them into doing something different.

Competition

It may come as something of a surprise that adolescents often find themselves in competition with parents. No doubt you will have heard your parents talking to you and starting off with 'If I had your opportunities'. Much of family life may be taken up by your endeavours to prove that they are wrong about a particular point or by their trying to prove you wrong. If you have a younger brother or sister, you might see them vying for affection and attention from your parents.

You may have noticed that when you were young, although you may not have done many things well, when you did in fact succeed in even quite a small thing, you were heaped with praise from your parents. It may have seemed that you could never do that particular thing too often or too much. Now you may be noticing that you are doing certain things very well indeed, in fact even better than your parents do or ever could. Rather than the praise which you were used to, now do you detect a hint of envy in them? How often are you accused of being big-headed? Or getting too big for your boots?

Graham the handyman

Graham had always been interested in doing things around the house. When he was 4 his prized Christmas present was a toy set of tools. He soon graduated to construction kits and, by the time he was 13, had his own 'adult' tool box. He started metalwork and woodwork at college and was looking forward to further education in some technical skill.

His father had always been a keen 'do-it-yourselfer'. Ward-

66

robe units were fixed, shelves were put up, chimneys were taken down, the house was redecorated. When Graham was young, his father always made time to show him how to do things and valued his assistance and praised him to his friends and neighbours as being proficient in the extreme for his age. 'Do you know that Graham hung that bit of wallpaper all by himself and measured it and put it up exactly right?' was just the sort of thing that he would say.

When Graham was 16, the family engaged in a massive redecoration of the house and he and his father set to, planning what to do. But the relationship had soured. They found it more difficult than usual to agree on any joint plan of action. Graham suggested one way of tackling something and his father suggested something else. The disagreements got worse and ended in arguments and rows, once with Graham storming out saying, 'Measure that yourself! Do it on your own!'

Graham returned some time later and set about putting up some shelves. His father at first offered to help but Graham refused. His father then started to give some advice on how to put the shelves up. Graham lost his temper and wrenched the bracket off the wall. 'That's it,' said his father. 'I don't want any more of your help. You keep your cleverness for school. I'll do this myself.'

It was on a Saturday when they were watching a tennis match at Wimbledon that Graham said to his father 'Do you know that man? His coach is 47 and he obviously must be able to thrash him at tennis, but still he says that he wouldn't be able to win because his coach has so much still to teach him.' His father laughed and said 'Come on, son, we have watched enough tennis, let's get on with the shelves.'

Brothers and Sisters

We are very keen on clear lines of authority and emphasise again and again that parents are in charge of the home and where their children are. But age does make a difference to the amount a parent delegates. If you are a single parent, you are already aware of how much you use your adolescent in caring for your younger children. All parents delegate some authority to their eldest child. Rules are different for them. Remember how useful they are for babysitting.

It is not only over differentials in rules and privileges that brothers and sisters fall out. They do it over sharing and many other aspects of their relationships: sharing a room, use of the bathroom, feeling bullied, feeling picked on, laughed at, never being left in peace. The feelings that can be generated over these issues . . . we do not need to tell you about them. Anyone who is not an only child may know what murderous feelings are like. (And only children can feel murderous about other people too.)

What to do about it? If you are one of the children or if you are a parent, remember that it ends, and sometimes even a few months make a lot of difference. If you are 14 and your 10-year-old brother is driving you mad and your parents are not doing anything about it, try to find two people of 25 and 21 and see what differences you can spot between them. Your parents may even have a similar age gap.

Parents, your children will always demand that you are fair and just. Do remember that it is an impossible expectation to fulfil. When you arbitrate between two of your children, your solution will be one that both dislike or one of them dislikes.

Other Relatives

Adolescents are able to choose their friends but have no control whatsoever over what relatives they have. We make four categories of other relatives – cousins, aunts and uncles, grandparents and 'old family friends'.

If your cousins happen to be teenagers themselves, especially if they are slightly older than you are, the advantages that you can get from that relationship are obvious. Aunts and uncles are almost bound to take your parents' side. Grandparents are different. They experienced your own parents when they were difficult as children and adolescents. They will therefore be more sympathetic to any complaints you have to make about how difficult your parents are. They are less caught up with parent/child things. They may share with you what worked with them when they were worried about your parents and you may notice that they can talk to your parents as no one else can.

George and the family reunion

George and his father were in the throes of a long-standing argument about whether he should give up his paper round in order to concentrate on his O-levels when the grand family reunion took place. All his father's parents' grandchildren were there. All nine of them. His grandfather was very quiet and hardly said a thing, but his grandmother attempted to organise the most minute detail. She wished to have all the grandchildren in one room so that they would enjoy each other's company. All the adult generation were to be with her and her husband in the other room where they were to be given tea and to make polite conversation.

George was saved from being overwhelmed by an event he thought was awful, by realising from the looks on his cousins' faces that they were just as fed up about meeting him and his sisters. Each family group of teenagers stayed together in separate parts of the room. George, to his surprise, found that he actually chose to stay with his sister on this social occasion. She had a useful function.

Later, a noise was heard in the next room. It was their grandmother, in raised voice, criticising one of the adults for his behaviour. Gradually George realised that it was his own father who was being criticised. Then, to his greater surprise, he heard his father retort in raised voice and with an expression of pique which he had never before noticed but which sounded vaguely familiar.

On the journey home in the car, George's father said 'Well, it wasn't too ghastly was it?'

'No' replied George, 'Grandma says we are going to do it again at Christmas.'

'Over my dead body,' retorted his father.

Nothing more was said about it and later on that weekend

George found his father receptive to the idea that he change his paper round for a Saturday job.

Grandparents see their grandchildren through a generation gap twice over. When they criticise their grandchildren's behaviour and blame it on the new and different way that their parents have been bringing them up, they ought to pause and realise what they are doing. If the younger generation's behaviour can be blamed on their parents, then grandparents carry some responsibility. They might remember that most people learn much of their parenting from their own parents.

Things that your grandchildren do that cause their parents difficulty, might be different from the sort of things that your children did to cause you difficulty. But the effect these things have on their parents are very much the same sort of effect your children's behaviour had on you. Therefore the feelings, the difficulties, the anxieties and frustrations aroused are much the same.

Isobel's granddaughter

Isobel Johnson made a vow never to interfere in the way her children brought up theirs. The years went by and she saw her daughter condone behaviour that she would not have condoned in her own child at that age a generation before.

She made allowances for new times and modern ways of bringing up children. Her grandchildren were not all that badly behaved, but she could not help but wonder why their mother and father did not tell them off more often when they misbehaved at mealtimes or used bad language.

When her eldest daughter, Susan, was having problems with her daughter, Caroline, Susan came to her for advice for the first time. Her trouble was that Caroline was not doing her homework properly, wanting to go out and coming home late.

'What can I do, Mum? I've tried everything and she won't do anything that I say?'

Isobel replied 'Well, do you remember that time, I think it

was in your last year at school, when you got very friendly with that boy? He had a motor bike and I was terribly worried about what you might get up to with him and that you might get hurt. It all finished, didn't it?'

'Yes,' her daughter said. 'What did you do to make me stop?'

Her mother replied, 'You know I can't remember what it was that I did. I remember that I did do something and it seemed to work. I knew I just couldn't let it go on.'

Susan left her mother's house resolved that she must do something more with Caroline than just say nothing and let her get away with everything. She was too anxious for it to continue and whatever happened, she would not let it go on. She also wondered if, in 20 years' time, she would be like her mother and have forgotten the details of what she had done.

4

Family Leisure

Holidays

Holidays used to be such exciting shared events. While you parents were in charge of choosing places, you allowed the children to have the illusion of choice and to share in some of the planning and much of the anticipation. The children were happy to follow you, go where you chose and to share and enjoy the activities of your decision.

Now things have changed. They are not sure that they want to go with you. They are bored by some of the places that you contemplate. Even if you take them where there are many activities for teenagers, they say that they are the wrong sort of teenagers – too northern, or southern, or eastern or western, snobby or plebian. And what do you do when the only person your daughter wants to go out with turns out to be the lifeguard?

They used to enjoy all the activities which you chose for them. They liked cycling, swimming and surfing with you; and even enjoyed the visit to the ruined castle. Now they want only to sunbathe and have no energy for the rest. Often it seems that all they want to do on holiday is exactly the same as they do at home. It is a lot for parents to give up.

Angela: America or staying at home.

> The Hardings won a competition. An all-expenses-paid holiday for three weeks to America. Bill Harding was a self-

employed plumber and his wife Janet worked part-time in a shop. They had two children, Angela, 16, at a private school where she was preparing for national exams and Adam who, at 12, had just started secondary school where his teachers had been concerned about his disruptive behaviour in class.

When Janet announced that the family had won the competition, Bill and Adam were delighted but Angela did not look very pleased.

Janet said, 'Aren't you looking forward to going to America for three weeks, Angela?'

Angela replied, 'Well, you said last Saturday I did not have to go on holiday with you this year. You said I could go with my friends after my exams. I can't afford to spend time away now. I want to stay at home.'

Bill and Janet were a bit taken aback for Angela had always expressed an ardent interest in foreign travel and they had thought she would be delighted with the family's stroke of good fortune. Although they had not felt badly off, they had not been anticipating such a luxurious holiday. Unlike his sister, Adam was delighted, and particularly keen on missing three weeks of school.

In the ensuing weeks, there was much discussion between Bill and Janet about what to do about Angela and between them and her. Some of the family harmony was disrupted by rows and on two or three occasions the discussions ended with Angela, her mother, or both, in tears. The essence of the conflict was that while Janet felt anxious about leaving Angela in the house by herself, Angela said she was old enough to fend for herself for three weeks and she added that she could concentrate on working for her exams. On the other hand, the problems with Adam seemed to fade into the background and he seemed to be getting on much better with his mother and father.

Adam was very excited about the trip. Somehow or other it seemed that all their energy and worry over Angela had taken some of the heat off him.

The family usually had tea on Sundays with Janet's mother, who lived in the next village. Janet was surprised when her mother did not take her side in the argument and even said that she felt it was perfectly reasonable for Angela not to want to go to America but to stay at home to concentrate on her school work. Angela's pleasure at her grandmother's position was dimmed when she heard her solution to the problem:

'You can come and stay with me for three weeks.'

Angela was determined that she wanted to stay by herself. Everything each one tried to do seemed to make things worse and became a problem in itself.

In conversation with a friend at work, Janet mentioned how she felt caught between the anxiety about leaving Angela and not wishing to force her to come to America with them lest the holiday be made a miserable event for them all.

'What can I do. I am at my wits' end? We have thought of everything.'

Her friend replied, 'What about that expensive school you send her to? Could they look after her for three weeks?'

'I had not thought of that. Perhaps I could ask them. But, if I suggested it, Angela would say she did not want to go and stay there. She still would insist that she live by herself at home. Because we have got ourselves into this sort of thing at the moment, everything I say she rejects out of hand. She says that I am the same.'

'And what about Bill and Adam?'

'They are spending all their time planning this holiday. I have never seen them spend so much time together since Adam was a little boy. They are both loving it.'

'Well, what I think you've got to do, Janet, is to try and find out from the school if they would have her, because there could be a compromise. What you have got to do is try to give Angela the idea that she thinks that staying at the school, if it is possible, would be a good thing. I am sure you'll be able to work out some way of doing that.'

What Janet did was to find out from the school if they would have Angela. They said that was fine. They would be happy to have her living in for the three weeks and they felt that Angela would probably enjoy staying with them for that time. She could still see her friends and keep up some of her evening activities, like the Guides and the youth club. She could spend weekends with her grandmother if she wanted. Janet thanked them and said that she would be back in touch to see if they would be taking up the offer. She still had to speak to Angela:

'Look, we're arguing all the time and this has got to stop. Over the next few months, what is it that you want most?'

Angela replied, 'Well, I first want to do well in my exams.'

'All right, now I've got this idea. Why don't you take a piece of paper and write down all the possible places you could stay and the pluses and minuses of each of them. It will be like giving them marks. And then whichever place, according to you, not just me, has got the most pluses against the minuses, we both agree is where you will stay while Dad, Adam and I are away.' Angela agreed.

'I'll put all the places down.' These were:

1. Accompanying the family to America on holiday.
2. Staying in the family home by myself.
3. Living with Gran.
4. Living at school. (This was a surprise to Angela.)

At the end of the exercise, they counted up the pluses and the minuses against each place. It came out that staying at the school had the most pluses. Angela agreed that this would be the best place for her to stay, given that what she wanted to do most was do well in her exams.

Parties

Birthday parties in which your children enjoy your leadership and your participation in games go out with adolescence. Adolescents still want parties and they may still want you to organise them and pay for them, but then they want you to disappear, preferably out of the house. Even if your teenagers value their own home too much to have one in their own house, they are generally still keen to go to other people's parties.

Jessica and the slogan

One solution was to use a community centre hall. Jessica's friend's parents did that. When Jessica's parents went to collect her, they found very little light coming from the building and a group of rather sheepish-looking parents starting to congregate in the entrance hall of the building. The way into the main hall was barred by a thick curtain over which was a large poster with the slogan 'Parents Keep Out'. The host parents were offering drinks with laughter in their voices.

Jessica's parents peeped and saw a disco with coloured lights and with 12-year-old children dancing, many in close embrace. They thought that the slogan communicated two things. It communicated one thing to the parents but, by accepting it, the parents communicated another thing to the young teen-agers. It was as if there was another slogan written big in that hall and it said 'Do what you like and you have our approval.' But this was not the time for confrontation with the hosts. Jessica's mother opened the curtain so that Jessica might see that she was there and they took her home in a few minutes.

5

School

Because people understand things differently at different ages we were worried that you might get the idea that we do not think school work is terribly important. Well, we do. It is important for you and for your future. We do not mean to be patronising and we do not want to give the impression that we think things are easy for you. We know about youth unemployment and that we are open to the accusation that we have got jobs and do not know what it is like to be young today. We acknowledge that we, along with your parents, have helped create this system in which you find yourself. We know that not everybody can go to university or become lawyers, doctors or bricklayers. We also know that, given the state of the world today, it may not be possible even to work on a car assembly line, or down a mine, or in a factory, or become a dustman. We have come to see life as unfair and unequal. School offers you a whole range of experiences. You can find out more about yourself as a person. At the very least it is a good testing ground to discover how you are going to manage the things that come up in life as you grow up.

It is difficult to recognise that, after your parents, your teachers are the next group of adults who have the most influence on your lives. You may be surprised to hear how much we still think about our teachers from our days in school. As with any other group of people who are important to you, you must learn what is the best way of influencing them. You will be surprised how little it takes to have them appreciate you and for you to develop a good relationship with them. Nobody wants to be teacher's pet or be accused by classmates of 'sucking up'. You will probably realise that most teachers do not like this either. Most teachers like their pupils to be questioning and challenging but also co-operative.

You may be surprised to hear that we feel restrained in these ways too, even in our adult life. Each of us is a member of a profession which has its own organisation, groups and sub-groups, which have influence on us in many ways: sending us work, giving us grants of money or helping us or our protegés to get jobs. We are also still not secure enough in our lives to dispense with the positive reinforcement of approval. We have gone through periods of being extremely rebellious and have fought with those in authority over us. We abandoned that attitude when we discovered that we were not getting what we wanted. We became more strategic. We found that we could get what we wanted, and still be thought of well enough by those in authority, and the compromise was not too great. But the awful realisation was that freedom, total freedom, just did not exist. Or if it does, we have not been able to find it.

Both of us have experienced someone in authority, whom we respected, criticising the way we presented ourselves. Our earlier rebellion, however, has turned to conformity when we have seen the positive effect it has had. We have realised there were many things we wanted from those people in authority that we felt would be useful. We started to see the way we presented ourselves as being important and as part of how we influenced our professional colleagues and the people that we became involved with. We changed, became more conventional and found that, not only other professionals noticed us more and in a different way, but that people we were employed to help became more open to us. This helped us to help them. We had become strategic.

So if your teachers complain about earrings or pink hair or

chains or whatever is the current style, ask this question, 'In 10 years' time shall I still be wearing pink hair and heavy earrings and wearing chains; and if so, what shall I be doing presenting myself in this way?'

Hair styles presented us with a similar issue. One of us, since adolescence, had had very short hair. He was determined to maintain this throughout his life, however bald or grey he became. Then quite suddenly there came a new movement in our society called skinheads, and short hair or none at all was associated with violence. Not liking this association, he put aside his wish for short hair in order not to be confused with being part of this movement.

Of course it is all ridiculous really. We remember the school teacher who would not take a punk on a school outing but would take the skinhead. When he was confronted about this by a colleague and his attention drawn to the punk person's philosophy of racial harmony and tolerance and the skinhead's philosophy of violence, he retorted, 'Well, that is all very well but I should feel very uneasy about somebody with coloured hair being in my party whereas somebody with very short hair, well that seems right for a young man. That is how we used to have our hair in the RAF.'

Adrian and the family life project

Adrian's home life was going through a sticky patch. His mum and dad had been rowing a lot and his dad had recently left home. This coincided with a project that he had to do for his social studies course on family life. He found it very difficult to deal with some of the theory that was being taught. His social studies teacher was quite an authoritarian and expected work to be done. Previously Adrian had not let him down and the work had been produced. The teacher was unaware of Adrian's home background and kept going on at Adrian about producing the work and telling him that he would not pass his work for CSE grades unless it was completed, that it was well within his capabilities and he was just being lazy by not doing it.

Adrian shared the problem with his best friend, who was the only person he felt he could talk to about what was going on. Although by this time his dad had come back home, things were still very difficult and he felt unable to write for his project without a whole lot of emotions coming up and over-whelming him. His friend said, 'Well, why don't you just tell Sparks what is happening? He will have to understand.'

Adrian said 'I can't talk to him. He is not the sort of person you can talk to. He will just shout at me and go on at me and we shall get into a row and I shall end up in even bigger trouble. So what, if I fail my CSE, I'll fail it. It is no big deal.'

Then his friend had another idea. 'Sparks is casting for the annual pantomime. As usual he wants people for the bit parts. There are never enough people to do those because no one wants to hang around at rehearsals. Why don't you volunteer and if you do that he will be impressed with you and he will get off your back about the project?'

Adrian thought that was a good idea and volunteered for the annual pantomime. It was during the two or three evening rehearsals that he began to see a different side to Mr Spark-brook and found him much more approachable.

Adrian still did not discuss his difficulty with his teacher, but to his surprise – and he never was able to work out how or why – he found that his project work became easier.

Shaun: swimming or the cadet force

Shaun joined the cadet force because he thought it might make his chances of getting into college that much better, but after a couple of terms he realised that it was interfering with his swimming. He did not want to offend the cadet-force master because his recommendation might be helpful to him later on, so he worked out with his friend Bill what to say to the master. He had a problem, he would say, because he enjoyed the cadet force and had become quite proficient at drill but now found that his swimming was losing out. He didn't want to leave the cadet force but he wanted to polish up on his swimming. He felt that if he didn't go to the cadet force for a few terms, he could catch up with some of the drill later on, but that if he did not do more swimming practice then his chances of being in the team would really go completely. And he had found it particularly helpful what the cadet master had told him about constantly working at the things he wasn't good at. Furthermore, the master had told him about genius being 1 per cent inspiration and 99 per cent perspiration.

Shaun therefore reframed his wish to leave the cadet force as a sacrifice and nobody was too hurt by it.

Teachers and your Pupils

You have chosen to become a teacher. Unlike some occupations, such as mining or working in a factory which may be the only employment available in an area, teaching represents a choice. Teaching is still called a vocation. That you are teaching and where you are doing it are your choices. Of course, you may feel frustrated with your rate of pay, that you are not teaching in the setting that you would choose, or by your prospects of career development. On the other hand your pupils have less choice. They are there by Act of Parliament at least until they are 16. You may have noticed a difference in your relationship with your students when they stay on after school leaving age.

We suggest an exercise: make a note of what you feel your relationship to be with some of your pupils, a month before they take their national exams at 16. Then, a month into the new term, review what your relationship is with those who have stayed on. Have those few months alone made a difference?

However, just because adolescents have got to be in school does not mean they are not motivated. They may still want to make the most use of the experience they have with you.

We hope you are aware of how very important and significant you are to your pupils. They have special names for you, they talk about you, they are interested in your private lives. They are interested in your relationships with each other. Remember how important your own teachers were to you. Perhaps you still think about them sometimes.

You will be used to adolescents being critical of anybody whom they feel is unfair. Now their view of what is fair and unfair may be, in its own turn, unfair, but they do seem to have a highly critical sense of what should and should not be done. Despite all the evidence to the contrary, adolescents expect everyone to keep all their promises. They are intolerant of human frailty when it is in adults. The trouble is that very often they interpret something that you may say or do, as a promise given, though you may not mean it as such. No doubt you have often been involved in conversations such as:

'You said I could.'

'No I didn't.'

'Yes you did, you said that if I did so and so I could do such and such.'

'No, I didn't say that. You didn't get what I meant at all.'

'Oh no, you are just saying that. You are being unfair.'

Things that we joke about, they take as deadly serious.

We have often talked about authority and using it creatively. Teachers have a very particular position with their use of authority. They must use it in ways that are very often difficult for other people to consider. For instance, have you ever thought of the effect of wearing a tiny CND badge on your jacket or dress? We suggest that this seemingly minor gesture of your political or private views could have quite a profound effect on your pupils in the message you are giving them about your stance on authority. We are not saying it is right or wrong to wear CND badges and we are not saying it is right or wrong to make your political views open to your pupils, nor to support CND. In our professional practice we made it our custom to have no outward sign of our feelings that could possibly be interpreted as being anti-authority. We felt that if we did not do this we should appear to adolescents as phoney and it would be an unnecessary diversion from a task that we and they have on hand, which is to help them through their adolescence leaving as much of their developing individuality intact as possible. And, of course, you teachers know how easy it is for adolescents to divert you from what you are trying to do with them. How many times in your classroom have you been trying to teach them a certain subject when something else has come up and you have gone off at a tangent? We think that if we show them some sign of anti-authoritarianism, like the wearing of a political badge, it will be seen either as (a) pretending to be on a side which we are not really because we are adults or (b) as ineffectual because we have not changed the world.

Walter, Brian and Glen: three generations of doctors

The Abbots were doctors. Walter Abbot had been a respected surgeon and was overjoyed when his son Brian got into medical school. Later, however, he was appalled when he heard from Brian that he had joined the young socialists. Throughout his time at medical school, Brian's father often spoke about doctoring but almost always this became an argument about their political views. However, after Brian had graduated, joined a successful general practice and become a family man, Walter felt differently about his son and was able to speak about him proudly as a success.

Their political discussions had a much more amiable air to them as time went on. Brian had gone to a boarding school, but his own son Glen went to the local comprehensive. He was a hard worker and applied himself to his studies. He got some fairly decent O-level results due to his hard work and his application. Brian was overjoyed and never doubted Glen's future career path, paying little heed to the teachers who felt that Glen's hard work and application had got him the results rather than any natural flair or brilliance. Glen then went into his period of study for his A-levels. He sat the exams and got through with moderate passes. Brian was disappointed but felt it had been a quirk of fate or examination nerves, that Glen was not feeling right on the day. Brian's solution was simple. Glen would just do an extra year at school and re-sit the exams. But Walter, Glen's grandfather had another idea. He would approach the dean of their old medical school and argue the case for Glen, despite his poor results.

'Look, our family has had long associations with that school and I am sure that the dean, who is an old friend of mine, will accept young Glen into the school. He knows that the Abbots are doctors and Glen will make a fine one.'

Brian would not countenance such patronage, however. 'My son will get into that school by his own efforts. He'll get those results.'

Meanwhile, Glen had decided what to do. 'Look, Dad, you're disappointed about my A-level results. Well, I'm very pleased about them. Quite frankly, I never dreamed I should get three A-levels at all. I have got them by really working hard and applying myself. I can't work any harder. I can't know any more. My brain is not the sort of brain that can take that sort of stuff. I can't imagine learning more and more complicated things than these subjects and which I'd have to if I was to become a doctor. What I'm going to do is to apply to join the army. They will give me a commission and I can get a degree and put to use my skills. You know they are mostly practical.'

Glen had reframed his own 'failure' into a success . . . He had decided to be himself. 'I am me.' But it was not without the expenditure of great energy. The confrontation with his father had been painful. It felt a very big step for him to go his own way. Brian, for himself, began to wonder if it was even as difficult for him to let his son Glen be 'me' as it had been for his own father, Walter, to let him have his socialist views. His feelings of pride in his son's resoluteness were mixed with his feelings of disappointment that his son's academic level and choice of career were not what he had wanted for his son.

He remembered his own father's joy at his becoming a medical student and distaste of his political allegiance.

Pauline and the classroom graffiti

Pauline and William's teenage daughters' parents' evening had a new arrangement this term. They were invited to go to their children's classroom for a group discussion between parents and teachers. Mounting the stairs they noticed how the school had changed since a few years before when they had first visited it. There were broken plaster on the pillars of the staircase and occasional graffiti on the walls. The classroom was also different. Each desk was almost black with ballpoint pen markings. Many of the coathooks on the wall were bent or broken off. Swear words and obscenities, some of them five inches high, were written on the walls.

That was what Pauline and William noticed when they went into the room, but the teachers talked with them about syllabus, attendance and homework. None of the other parents mentioned anything about the state of the room, but a few minutes before the meeting was due to close, Pauline could contain herself no longer. Like a child she held up her hand and said, 'There is something I really must say.' She felt herself getting hot and anxious, as if she was a naughty pupil herself, but persevered and said 'I really am very concerned about the state of this room and the state of the school. It seems to have deteriorated so much since we came on our first visit.'

'Oh, yes, of course,' said the form teacher and gave the collected parents a lecture about government policy, financial cuts and the delay in the redecoration programme. Pauline, ignoring disapproving glances from William, said, 'It may be down to my confusion or not being able to see things clearly, but I am having difficulty in seeing the link between government cuts and the obscene graffiti on the walls. Why is it there?'

The teacher replied, 'Well, because we don't know who has done it. Not only your children use this classroom, but because of the school's open-door policy, any children from any other classroom can come into it.'

Pauline said, 'I am sorry but I still can't see why it is still on the walls. Why has it not been cleaned up?'

The teacher replied, 'I am sure you would like the children to clean it up themselves. we think that is a good learning experience.'

Said Pauline, 'But they haven't done it. Which is the better learning experience for them, waiting for them to clean it up or leaving it on the walls for them to be confronted with it every day? It is like saying to them, "This is OK to do".'

The teacher then said, 'Well, the caretaker refuses to clean it up because he says he is fed up with it, and I don't have time to do it myself.'

Pauline responded, 'I know it is easy for me to ask why it has not been done and that you are the one who has to deal with it, but I have a suggestion. There are 22 of us here at the moment. If you can lay your hands on cleaning materials, I suggest we clean the classroom now ourselves.'

The other parents, silent up to this point, started muttering. One said that she did not find it offensive but others said they strongly supported Pauline. The teacher said they could not allow the parents to do the cleaning but had got the message. As they were leaving the room, one of the other parents, a man who had said nothing during the meeting, came up to Pauline and muttered, 'You know the school motto: "In place of discipline, let's talk about it"'.

A few days later Pauline's daughter reported that the children had cleaned the walls, albeit not very efficiently.

Use of your First Name

Can you, as a parent or teacher, also be a friend to your child or pupil? Let us start an exploration of this idea by looking at how you address each other. The traditional way for children to address their parents is to call them 'Mother' or 'Father', 'Dad' or 'Mum'. They call their teachers Mr, Mrs, Miss, or Sir, and in our experience people have got on one way or another with these forms.

Some current thinking suggests that, because you are people and they are people, you should be open to having your pupils address you by your first names as you do them. We liked some of the ideas in, of all things, an Edwardian book called *How to deal with Lads* by the Revd Peter Green.

With regard to the boy's attitude to you, I would say be as friendly as possible, but do not allow the slightest rudeness to pass. I once knew a man who let his boys call him 'Billy' to his face. I don't believe boys care a bit more, or indeed as much, for a man in such cases, and I am sure it is wrong in principle.

86

If they are insolent to you, it may pass, but if they are encouraged to be insolent in a wider world to others, or their social superiors, they will suffer for it. If a boy is insolent to me, I say quietly 'Ned, you forget yourself. Please remember to whom you are speaking. I don't like such manners.' You will not have to say such a thing twice, either to the same boy or to others of the group, and the boy will bear no malice.'

Of course, Mr Green's language and his terms of 'his social superiors' might be questioned today, but we take 'social superiors' as meaning those who have a higher place in the social structure, in the hierarchy of status, age or responsibility. This includes parents and teachers.

We like the distinction that Peter Green makes between being, as he puts it, 'as friendly as possible', and being their friends.

We put forward the view that it is important to have a clarity of relationship with an adolescent. This includes not treating as an adult someone who is not an adult. A much-put-forward notion is that you can be friends with your child or friends with your school pupil. We feel that this is not possible. 'Close the generation gap at all costs' is the cry. 'Why?' Our view is that the attempt to close the generation gap and to define the relationship as being something it is not confuses the adolescent in an already confusing world. You cannot be both a parent and a friend. You are either one or the other. You cannot be both a schoolteacher and a friend. You must be one or the other.

'I am not a fan of rigidity or of distant, authoritarian parenting. But I see a great many pseudo-sophisticated children who need parents and not tall pals' wrote Ellen Goodman, a columnist with the *Boston Globe*.

Of course, there are elements in a relationship between friends that are common to the relationship between a parent and a child, and a child and a teacher at school. Just because you are *friendly* does not mean that you are friends. It is our view that adolescents prefer this to be clear.

Paul Watzlawick, an American writer, put forward the point that the generation gap which has existed for thousands of years only becomes a problem when people try to close it.

Remember, many adolescents actually like the gap. One of the things that usually makes them cringe with embarrassment is when schoolteachers or parents try to over-identify with them, their lifestyle, their fashion, or their music.

> In one seminar we were running, an adolescent speaking about the generation gap said 'No, I do not like it, but perhaps it has got to be there. You know I really enjoy having a bath and filling it right up to the overflow and lying in it, and how I hate the hard edges of the bath against my elbows and heels. But where would my bathload of water be without those edges.'

Homework and Exams

Of course you are going to be in conflict about this: conflict between the pressures of studying, with the other things in life that you are interested in and enjoy; conflict between yourself and your parents. The trouble with your parents' generation is that they do have a point of view and they do have a larger experience. Try as you may you cannot deny that they have been through adolescence and are now in adulthood. They have been in school and they have had some life after school and they can see the links. They can make the links between their life at school and their life after school: you can only guess at them.

Your teachers too were adolescents and faced these pressures. You may conclude that they did do their homework, otherwise they could not have become teachers.

But what advice can you get from them? You don't want to be told 'Just do your homework' because just being told to do it is not enough. They might be able to tell you how they dealt with the sorts of conflicts which you have to face, when they were your age. Try asking them.

Melanie: should she study?

Melanie was approaching her O-levels and her mock examination results were terrible. 'I am not going to go through with this', she said to her parents. 'I am going to give up school, it is a waste of time. What is the point of going through with it, I am only going to fail. Even if I pass and get a few, I am soon going to be on the dole when I leave.'

Her parents had hoped that she would continue at school, do her A-levels and go to university. They spoke to her, entreated with her, cajoled her, threatened her, shouted at her, all to no effect. And the more they went on about it, the more she seemed to have dug her heels in and refused to carry on at school. They enlisted the help of an old family friend, who was himself a university graduate, to speak to Melanie about the benefits of education and, in particular, the job prospects afterwards. He had a half-hour chat with Melanie that she found only slightly less embarrassing than he did himself. At her boyfriend's house that evening, her boyfriend heartily congratulated her on her decision to leave school. 'School is a waste of time,' he said to her. 'You are much better off leaving, getting a job – you would probably get a job in that factory down the road, no trouble at all.' His own parents agreed and said, 'Yes, what you want to be concentrating upon is getting a job and, hopefully, in a couple of years' time, getting engaged and then married. What do you want to read books for, a girl of your age has got better things to do than reading books – they are a waste of time.'

Melanie went home and started to study. Her parents, noticing the change, said to her 'Was it Ken's talk with you that made the difference?' She smiled.

How to Study

There are now a few good books about this subject and we recommend some at the end of this book. We have been helped. Our whole way of studying and planning our work was revolutionised by workshops which we attended. This book is 'homework' to us, for we have done nearly all of it in our spare time in the evenings.

So it is not for us to say how to study except to share some of the things which we have found really helpful.

Do it regularly, an hour a day is better than three hours every two or three days.

Start early in the year.

Have goals that are small and easily measured; give yourself the incentive of a treat when you have realised one of them – even a small goal for that evening (we treated ourselves to a swim after we had finished one draft of this book).

Make links with the rest of your life.

If you find this last suggestion difficult, then think again.

Ashley: studying and hairdressing

Ashley wanted to be a hairdresser and she and her father were in conflict time and again about her study. Her ambition to enter hairdressing had been accepted by the family, but not her wish to opt out of her last year's school work.

'What is the use of any of this for me in my profession', she said.

'Test me', retorted her father.

'All right, French?'

'Some of the best hairdressers are French or pretend to be French. It would be impressive for your clients if you could actually speak some, especially if they were French tourists.'

'All right, history?'

'Women's fashion has been a subject of study for a long time. That is history as well, the history of hair fashions. The difference between how Cleopatra had her hair and Anne Boleyn, for instance. They are interesting things and would be a useful subject for you to study. I think it should be at college that you would study things like this. Get in some good practice now.'

'OK then, this will stump you, what about chemistry? What is the use of chemistry?'

'All those hair lotions that you use on people's heads and shampoos. Isn't it useful to know how chemicals can damage people's hair. I am sure that is an essential part of your hairdressing training.'

'OK then', she said, 'you have got an answer for everything.'

Finally, do try to make it all as interesting as possible for yourself. If you study best with music, have music. If you study best with silence, have silence. If you like pictures and colours, use them. If you do not, then ignore them.

Exams

In examination preparation and sitting, the strategic approach comes into its own more acceptably than in perhaps any other area of life. The idea of examination technique has been accepted for many years. Look at old papers, study old questions, perform 'role-play' in the form of dummy answers for dummy exams. Your whole mock exams are a strategy, are they not?

When you look at the questions on the paper, rank them first in the order of your competence to do them and bear that in mind when you plan the order in which you are going to answer them. Remember that passing an exam is a matter of scoring points. It may be better to get 50 per cent of question A and 70 per cent of question B than 100 per cent of question C. Remember every little thing for which you can get a point, such as every little bit of extra information.

Finally, you might find it helpful to think that the examiner is on your side, to think that the examiner really wants to pass you. Help him.

6

Careers

Choices

Schooling is largely about choices. The local education department will have chosen what sort of schooling to provide in your area. Your parents will have decided to which school to send you. Your teachers have decided where to work, how and what they are going to teach and how they are going to run the school. What choices do you have?

You may have had some say in your parents' decision about the choice of school. You may have had some say in decisions about which subjects to continue to take for examinations. You will have chosen in which extra-curricular activities to participate, which games, which clubs, which outings. You have made choices about friends, who to seek out and who to reject. These choices are part of deciding how you are best going to spend your time in this place that somebody else has chosen for you to be in.

How much you are going to concentrate on what the teachers say? How hard you are going to study? How much you are going to enjoy the experience? How much time will you allocate to homework, to friends, to listening to records, to games? You choose whether to work hard or to make your very good subjects perfect or to spend some more time in making your less successful subjects a little bit better. You choose how much time you spend on experimenting with sex or experimenting in the chemistry laboratory.

These decisions, some of which have already been made

by you or other people, will probably influence the rest of your life. There is not the slightest chance of knowing what would have happened if the choices had been different.

If you lived in a society which said that education was not compulsory . . .

If the education department had decided to have a totally comprehensive system rather than a system of grammar schools and secondary schools . . .

If your parents had decided to send you to X House school rather than G comprehensive school . . .

If you decided to take history, metalwork and physics in your examinations instead of woodwork, geography and mathematics . . .

The choice has been made and the most you can get from it in the future is to think how you made it and how it affected you.

Employment

We find it hard to say anything about jobs without appearing patronising. Bear with us. We readily admit the obvious. As we have said to your parents, we both have jobs which we enjoy and which pay us fairly well. We have no complaints on either of those scores. We wonder if you would believe us if we tell you that when we were your age we never imagined that we should be doing these things and certainly not that we should ever be writing this sort of book. We often wonder how it all came about. Certainly our first ambitions were high but in quite unrelated spheres – to be an international racing driver, an entertainer, or just to get out of the country. And when we started our present professions our ambitions and expectations were to 'heights' far lower than those which we have achieved.

In both cases we chose our first jobs simply as the only way we could think of to leave home.

In our youth, the link between school and work was very

strong. One followed the other automatically. Today it is different.

Fairness and Competition

In families things are usually shared equally. Each has a similar helping at dinner; each has the same amount spent on clothes or on education or on Christmas presents. This is how it should be. Some people think that this is how society should be. We do not want to enter that debate but merely emphasise that society is not like that. In societies there are differences. Therefore there are things which are fair and things which are unjust. There is competition. In Britain it is warmer in the south than in the north. Some diseases are more common in one area than another. In our lifetime there have never been enough jobs to go around.

As an adolescent you will have carried the banner of fairness. We do not wish to discourage you from carrying it but ask you to be cautious lest when you leave school and are entering your working life you make it into a cross.

We have found it quite helpful in our own thinking to limit our goals. Rather than trying to make society fairer, we have concentrated on trying to make ourselves more fair, and trying to make small changes. If we can be fairer in ourselves and especially fair to ourselves, then we think we have made some progress.

If you want to become an airline pilot, have worked hard academically to obtain all the necessary qualifications and then you find yourself having trouble with your eyesight, you will consult an optician. If the optician tells you that you need glasses, you will feel that this is unfair. Indeed it seems unfair that your parents have slipped up in how they made you.

But the first fairness should always be to yourself. You may realise that your first job need not be your only job. One of the things that is easier to do today is to take time off for wide experience and travel or to do something else. There are many careers, our own included, in which this is seen as a positive advantage in recruitment.

One of the differences in your generation is that being unemployed is not such a stigma now as it was in the past. If you are unemployed nowadays, people are likely to feel sympathy towards you, rather than to feel that you are a shirker.

Interview Techniques

There are many books published today about interview techniques. We suggest that you try some out. Most schools have some video equipment. If your teachers have not thought of it already, do a role-play of an interview with the video and play it back. Try playing the role of yourself being interviewed and do try playing the role of the interviewer, attempting to find out about you.

Decide what things about yourself you are prepared to share, and which ones especially so. What sort of impression do you want to make? What sort of questions or anxieties are likely to be in the minds of interviewers? What will they be looking for and what will they be concerned about? How can you help them? Think of interview as meaning what it says. It is a view between two people – they are interviewing you and you are interviewing them.

When anybody asks us for advice, we always say two things – one is to sit well back in your chair and the other is to expect the unexpected question.

7

Conflicts and Sanctions at Home

What Affects Families and who to Blame

Families are a collection of individuals who relate to each other and with each other.

The traditional or usual way of explaining events is to blame something. A is blamed for causing an effect on B. This idea of cause and effect is like a straight line between two points. We have found it more helpful to use a circular way of explaining behaviour in families.

Family members are interdependent. Individual members have certain personalities and certain attributes. The way they are affects others. A relationship between A and B has an effect not only on each other but also on a third party C. C, in turn, also has a relationship with A, and the relationship between C and A affects B, and so on. To summarise: the way I am affects the way you are, and the way you are affects the way I am.

Many people have come to us with their stories about their family life. We always learn from them. Often they want to ask us one question. It is a question about blame.

Now you may have gathered already that we are very keen on seeing people as responsible for their own actions. This does not mean that we see people as also being responsible for what other people do in response to their actions. So when parents ask 'Am I to blame?' or 'Is John's drug-taking or overdosing or glue-sniffing because I divorced my husband?' we always say that that is not the way we see things.

'Well are you saying then that I am not to blame?' We again say that that is not the way we see things.

We do not think in terms of people being blamed or innocent. If another question following on from that is, 'Well is it wrong for me to feel guilty about what I have done?' we should respond 'Feeling guilty is feeling guilty, it is neither wrong nor right. It is a feeling that you have.'

'But I should like to stop feeling guilty.' Then we should say 'We might be able to help you in that area. But first we need to work out with you some way in which you will be able to decide when you have stopped feeling guilty.'

Chris's music

Chris's parents had bought him a new hi-fi for his birthday. He got great enjoyment playing his records on it. He liked his music loud.

Soon a battle developed: Chris would put his record player on and within the half hour his mother would complain to him about the loudness. Chris's response was not to do anything about it. His mother would tell him to turn the hi-fi down again. Chris would still not pay any attention, but would say something to her like 'Leave me alone, it is not that loud.' This would continue until Chris would shout at his mother and they would be involved in a row.

At this point his father would intervene and tell Chris not to be so rude to his mother, that he would take the hi-fi away so that he would not be able to use it. In fact that was what he was going to do right now. At this stage, Chris's mother would say, 'Oh no, we don't need to go that far, do we?' and no more would be said until the next day when Chris would put his records on and his mother would start complaining. And so on.

Who is to blame for the continuing rows? Was it Chris playing his loud music or his mother for nagging, or Chris being rude or his father for intervening and threatening to take the hi-fi away? Or was it his mother for stopping his father from carrying out his threat? Or was it the hi-fi manufacturers for increasing the technology to such a state where it is so easy to play loud music on the cheapest of hi-fi sets? Or was it Edison for discovering how to harness electricity? Ridiculous you might say. Of course. Wondering too long about the question of who is to blame is not a very productive pastime.

Punishment, Penalty and Sanctions

We see punishment as the wilful infliction of physical or emotional harm on another person who is seen to have done morally wrong. We see penalty as the price paid for infringing a regulation. We see a sanction as a curtailment or limit on the availability of a resource.

Our view is that it is important in adolescence to challenge authority which administers punishment, penalty and sanctions. It is one of the ways in which adolescents test their environment, their structure and you. We suggest that you value the exercise and their need to engage you in it. It is a ritual with rules and tactics. Please do not worry what it is about.

Sanctions

Do not paint yourself into a corner. Once again we go back to *How to deal with Lads* by the Revd Peter Green who warned against adults' imposing a sanction which they might have to go back on and in that way became a stick to beat themselves with.

Facing one of the most dreaded things in a boys' club, when something serious has happened but nobody owns up, the leader makes a suggestion. If an extreme sanction, such as 'closing the club', is to be contemplated, then it should be done for a fixed number of days and not 'until the culprits own up'.

Be sure to say that the club will be shut for a certain time, say a week or a fortnight, if the names are not given in, and not to say that the club will be closed till names are in, or you may be in the undignified position of having to go back on your word in the event of the names not coming in at all.

In moments of stress and anger parents often paint themselves into a corner: 'Right, no pocket money for three weeks' or 'No going out this weekend'. This then may so often end up with the sanction being more difficult for you than for them, and impossible to maintain.

Sarah and vegetarian cookery

Sarah was fed up with lack of help from the teenagers in the household in washing-up and said that she would cook only vegetarian food until she got more help in the kitchen.
    This sanction could only have beneficial effects:
1. the diet would be better for her children
2. Sarah would learn about vegetarian cookery
3. the adolescents could be forced into cooking it for themselves
4. the adolescents could co-operate with the washing-up.

But if you catch yourself in a moment of fury, feeling that you must lay down the law, do try saying something like: 'Right, there will be consequences, that is definite. I shall decide them later.' Then, in the colder light of day, possibly in consultation with other adults or your own children, you can decide what the law is and how you are going to enforce it.

For teachers, the same: you will be most familiar with things happening in your classroom which nobody owns up to. The temptation either to ignore such things or to do something punitive to the whole class is probably about the same. On the whole we usually recommend that doing nothing should be avoided. We think it is better to show that you have noticed the transgression or breaking of the rules. If you are going to impose a sanction, then we suggest you bring all your creative powers to bear in imposing one that is going to have benefits rather than be simply retribution and punishment.

If the sanction that you impose is the denial of certain privileges, then we recommend Mr Green's advice of having a fixed, quantifiable limit to the sanction, either in terms of amount or time.

Lines must be drawn but sometimes it is best to draw them in pencil.

More about Rules

Sometimes it is important to let children know you have made a fuss. We have every sympathy with parents who do this. For example, the first time something happens: giving them a good shaking, getting in touch with the police if they are home very late, or getting obviously and very upset. We have talked about family rules and how they develop. The rule, Mum or Dad does nothing when . . . is all too easily established. Then when you do something you are breaking a 'rule' which you have made.

You might sometimes think about what other rules you have helped to make in your family. Some people's include: 'I will clear up after you'; 'I will rescue you'; 'You may dress and do your hair as you like'; 'I will pay your debts'; or, 'I will go to the teacher or speak to the boss'.

Knowing Where your Children are

You may have seen the television advertisement which shows an adolescent going out of the front door with the caption 'Do you know where he is tonight?' You may be interested to know that in some recent research the group of children who were least in trouble with the law were those whose parents could answer Yes to the television question.

We are not advocating that you adopt a secret police attitude, nor that you never let your children out. But do try to avoid it becoming usual for them not to tell you and for you not to know where they are. Let the milestones of staying out late, like 11.00 p.m. and midnight, be passed after much negotiating by them and serious thought by you. Avoid establishing the rule that all changes can be brought about easily, particularly those to do with limits, boundaries and what is to be permitted. If they continue to expect rapid change, they will get a nasty shock when they reach adulthood.

Lies

You will know that children lie. You will know that adults lie. Do not suppose adolescents are different. Fielding, a character in E.M. Forster's *Passage to India* 'dulled his craving for verbal truth and cared chiefly for truth of mood'.

Censorship and Age Restrictions

Do you select what books you leave lying about the house or what magazines are open? How much do you control what is shown on television? How would you respond if you saw that your children had hired a horror video and were watching it on your equipment? Do remember that we shall be asking you who paid. They may have paid for the hire of the video, but you have paid for the set and certainly pay the electricity bill.

What happens when you object to something they have bought? They counter with, 'Well, it is my money, I can do what I want with it. I have been the one going out on the paper round.'

There are several ways of dealing with this. One is ignoring it and saying, 'I don't accept your argument.' We suggest going back to our definition of adolescence and the issue of the dependence and independence. We suggest that you remind your adolescents that they are not totally independent of you as yet. If they wish with their money to buy things to which you object, then they must also remember that they are not spending their money on things such as food, heat and furniture. When they are in a position to do this, you will have no reply to 'It's my money, I can do what I want.'

We think that occasional censorship is no bad thing. We have had to do this often in writing this book. We cannot write as fast as we can talk, nor talk as fast as we can think. Something had to go and we had to decide what.

Sometimes bringing up a family is like tending a garden. It must be sown, nurtured and controlled. And you are never quite sure how it is going to turn out.

Gardens too are a load of missed opportunities. Not all the seeds germinate. The climbing rose grows this way and not that. The tree does inhibit the lawn. You do not spend your time in the garden lamenting how it might have been; you let those dreams go and enjoy it as it is.

Whose Body is it?

Fashionable oriental families used to bind the feet of their little girls so that they remained small into adulthood. Certain African tribes ritually scar teenagers. Some religious groups circumcise boys. Many people will see these as cruel acts.

What adolescents do to themselves can also be seen in this light. Tight shoes, into which some adolescents cram their feet, deform and may cause problems later. Their make-up may contain harmful chemicals. The dyes they use on their hair may ruin it. Ear piercing and tattooing are virtually impossible to reverse.

Discourage them. Try to keep making them wait for them. We think that that interaction between them and you is, rather like the censorship we mentioned earlier, no bad thing.

We also think that many of the wishes which adolescents have most strongly are wishes held only temporarily. The wish may have come and gone but, if acted upon, may have permanent consequences. You can be a punk for a while and suffer no lasting damage. But the same does not apply to tattoos or ear piercing.

We have tried to get you parents to look at things from the point of view of different ages. Perhaps you can try to ask your children the question: 'Last year, what did you really want that I would not let you have? Do you remember? Do you still want it?'

Political Stands

What do you do about your son's being a skinhead?

What do you do about the Nazi insignia and how do you deal with your father, who fought in the war, complaining about his grandson's wearing a symbol of the very thing that he detested and fought against? How do you explain it to your friends when you go to the Labour Party meeting? On the other hand, how do you explain to your friends at your club when they tell you that they have seen your son daubed with various left-wing political slogans, out collecting money for strikers or the latest topical cause?

No matter how much you recognise that adolescence is a time of rebellion and questioning of parents' values, and no matter how much you think this is healthy, you may still find it impossible to cope with views that you find detestable. You might be expecting us at this stage to say once again that there is nothing very much you can do about it. And of course to a certain extent we are. You must decide how much you are willing to support their actions. You might answer that you do not support their actions at all. But of course you are; you are housing them, feeding them, and you probably give them money with which they can support their particular ideologies. How far are you prepared to do this? Are you prepared to make a deal with them? Are you prepared to negotiate? Or will you deal only on the basis of principle?

Harry and the swastika

Harry, from India, had a lot of contact with some young lads who were involved in the skinhead National Front movement.

Because of his work he came into daily contact with them. Fed up with the continual taunts of 'Paki' and other derogatory terms, he found he could reconcile his professional work which was being involved with his revulsion at their professed ideology. He found it more and more difficult to put it down to adolescent rebellion.

What to do about them? The more he told them off about it, the more they did it, the more angry he got with them so it went on in a repeating cycle. Then he remembered his father's telling him about the origins of the swastika. He looked it up in the *Oxford Dictionary* and was surprised to find that the origin of the word was from the Sanskrit, meaning 'well-being, good or luck', and it was an ancient symbol. So he got a large badge with a swastika on it, put it on his jacket and went in the next day to the usual place where he met these boys.

He was greeted with hoots of surprise and derision. 'You can't be in the National Front, you are a Paki.' 'Of course I'm not in the National Front', he said. 'I am wearing it because I am a Hindu.' 'But you Pakis can't wear the swastika.' 'Of course we can, we were wearing it long before anybody who was a Nazi wore it, because the swastika is an ancient symbol of the Hindus; it is to do with their religion', he told them.

When they were confronted with this further, he showed them the definition in the dictionary. They did not stop wearing their swastikas, but they stopped taunting him, and his relationship with them improved.

Stuart and Fred: politics and tea

Stuart was fed up with his son Fred's constant preaching to him about his 'middle-class bourgeois' values and his non-recognition of socialism. He would get into row after row with him. His constant pointing out to his son that he was actually living a very middle-class, comfortable way of life, while having these values, did not seem to have any effect.

One day, Fred came back from school and tea was not laid at the table. When he queried this with his mother she said, 'Your father told me that he had been very impressed with what you said to him yesterday and we are donating all the money which we used to spend on tea, to some political cause that you have been telling him about.'

Fred was very impressed with this. To his surprise, he got the same message the next day and so on for a week or so and then it stopped. His relationship with his father improved; he did not lecture him so much because, surprisingly, his father started to talk to him and listen to him more. They had several impressive discussions, some passionate, but no longer did they have arguments.

Gratitude and Attitude

Parents very often complain about the adolescent's 'attitude'. It is very hard to pin them down on what they mean about this. Very often they talk about the adolescent's not being grateful for . . . for what? For all the things they do for them? For the facilities they have available? For all the things they do for bringing them into this world and giving them education, money, the sacrifices the parents make for them, and so on.

Louise's gratitude

Derek was fed up with Louise, his 15-year-old daughter, and her attitude. She seemed to be surly, taking everything for granted and never seeming grateful for any things she got. When asked about what she was interested in and what she was doing at school, at the slightest attempt to make some sort of conversation, she would clam up with monosyllabic answers. One evening Derek went into Louise's room, when she was doing her school work, to have it out with her.

'What are you doing?' he asked her.

'My school project on family life,' she said.

'Oh, can I have a look at it?'

'Yes, if you like,' she said.

This is what he read:

Gratitude

'You enjoyed making me, but you did not know you had done it until some time later. In the meantime I had to cope with being ignored. During that time I made a perilous journey into your uterus. I was tiny and needed blood but you organised a blood supply for me only just in time. You nearly aborted me but I withstood your neglect and survived. At my birth I nearly died but you complained of the pain and you just stood idly by. And afterwards you got drunk.

'In my infancy I was treated like an object. You praised me when I said my first words but you pushed me into doing everything before I was ready and I fell over and hurt myself many times.

'You made me very dependent on you, and yet abandoned me often in the evenings to be looked after by people you paid by the hour.

'I gave purpose to your life and to your marriage. I became a focus for your thoughts and your conversations. I made it easier for you to meet other people of your age and to make new friends. I completely transformed the relationship which both of you had with your own parents.

'You ask me to be grateful.

'I am sorry about my attitude.'

8

Sex

Have you realised that you now have the potential to turn your parents into being grandparents? Just think what that does to them. The next thing they will start thinking about is your leaving home.

Maria and parental curiosity

Maria tried everything with her first boyfriends. She would talk to them only on the doorstep outside the front door. She would take telephone calls only if she took the telephone right outside the kitchen and put a blanket over her head. She would rush to catch the post first so that nobody could see what she was receiving. And yet none of it seemed to work. She could not, try as she did, get rid of the conviction that her parents were intensely curious about what was going on. It was when she shared it with her grandmother who said, 'Yes, your mum was just the same' that she felt some of the pressure coming off. She decided that it was OK for her parents to be curious and that she could tolerate it.

Nick and his father

Nick found it very difficult when his father kept asking him about his girlfriends and asking what he got up to with them. He found his father's comments to his father's friends ('He's a big strong lad now, the girls have got to look out') to be acutely embarrassing and consequently he would not bring any of his girlfriends home. This continued until his latest girlfriend called for him at home and found him out. On his return Nick found her chatting apparently quite contentedly with his father, and he felt differently.

You will realise that your parents have just got to get used to your having sexual feelings. One of the things that you may get into a muddle about is the difference between sexual feelings and having sex. Your parents may be equally muddled. People have feelings that they do not act upon. Indeed, we have not come across anyone who has convinced us that he or she has not at some time in life had sexual feelings or fantasies about someone else which they have not acted upon.

Your parents will be concerned about what we shall be telling you about sex and you can be pretty sure that they will be reading this section. Should you be having sex or not? Should you have sex with more than one person? Or with more than one gender of person? Should you masturbate? Should you enjoy masturbating? How seriously should the age of consent be regarded?

What we are doing is talking to you about it; and we are able to do that while you are not able to reply. If you feel that you have got some answers to these questions, you may re-direct them to your parents. We have tried very hard to be neutral about most of the issues in this book and we hope that you have understood that if you have read other parts. In our experience, having sexual intercourse early rather than later increases the chances of there being problems in life. At the very least there is a strong link between early sexual intercourse in girls and the development of cancer of the cervix in later life. We do not mention this association to scare, merely to point out some of the risks. At your time of life, when there are so many difficult things to negotiate, our wish is that you should be spared the difficulties that active sexual relationships can bring. On the other hand, we think that it is very likely that the majority of you will disagree with this and will feel most strongly that you should be given more freedom to experiment to the full.

The only concrete advice we have to give to you, whether you experience emotional difficulties related to sex or not, is not to avoid educating yourself about these matters and specifically to find out all there is to know about contraception. Information about birth, about some of the technical aspects of sex, about physical dangers such as the sexually transmitted diseases (venereal disease), is readily available to people of your age these days.

We have heard some people say that sexually transmitted diseases 'should be cured' – that the National Health Service should research foolproof ways of curing all forms of them so that they cease to be a problem. The stark reality, however, is that medical science has failed to keep up with the newer forms of these diseases, just as the inventors and manufacturers of pesticides have failed to keep ahead of the new forms of resistance developed by insects.

Sex and Sexuality, Feelings and Actions

Parents find it difficult to think and talk about sexual feelings towards their own children. Even just reading these words might make you shudder, want to turn the page and go on to another section, or to put the book down completely. Wait a minute!

As we have just said, feelings are often seen as the same as actions. Our view is that anybody may feel a whole range of things. Further to that, our view is that there is no such thing as a bad or wrong feeling. Feelings are feelings. It is what we do with them, that is to say actions, that can cause some difficulty. Parents may have sexual feelings about their children. This is very different to many of the horrific cases of incest and child sexual abuse that you may have read about or seen television programmes about. We are not trying to put you in this category.

There are many ways of looking at the boundary between children and parents. Take the issue of nudity: do parents enjoy seeing their children's bodies and do they give them pleasure? Do parents let their children see them naked? Is this something they find disturbing, beneficial or something they do not think about? But it is a sexual issue which has to be dealt with.

Adolescent teenage girls may flirt with their fathers. This is a good way of testing yourself as a woman; your femininity can be tried out with a safe man. What better testing ground could there be than to try out behaviour like that with someone you feel safe with, to try it out with the man who made you? Fathers worry that they are reciprocating to this feeling of pleasure from their daughter's flirting with them. There might be instances of a daughter leaning over so that her breasts touch her father; or when she embraces him she might hold back, feeling some embarrassment. Or when a son greets his mother, she may sense his holding back so that her breasts do not touch him.

Parents may dream about their children, may have feelings or fantasies about them. They may also feel jealous about their children's associations with the opposite sex.

Homosexuality

It is illegal for homosexual acts to take place with a male under the age of 21. Like all things that are illegal, we advise you not to do it. We do not have such clear advice for girls for there is no legislation against female homosexuality.

Legalities apart, you, as parents and adolescents, may have a lot of feelings about the subject. We refer again to our emphasis that there is a difference between feelings and actions. Your sexual experimentation within the constraints of the law is your business. Homosexuality as a way of life is against the norm, be it biological, social or legal – however much you think it should not be. It will cause conflict and doubt and worry. In general, in our society, we advocate that you avoid making a commitment that goes against the norm until you are through adolescence. We should say much the same to you if you were deciding, at this age, on becoming a monk or a nun.

So what do you do if you are at a single-sex boarding school, or what do you do if someone of your own sex has made a sexual advance and you have found it exciting? First, we do not feel neutral about single-sex boarding schools, which we think are difficult places for growing up. While we should like you to experiment with your own sexuality we suggest it should not be too wide. Our views against too much heterosexual experience too early in emotional sexual development also hold here.

Do not feel alarmed or committed if you do experience sexual feelings towards members of the same sex. See them as another part of your repertoire of feelings. And you can decide later whether to act on them or not.

Parents, we know you might be worried about this, but do not be offended if we tell you that it really is not your business. We hope that your adolescent children will not be taking any irrevocable steps in this direction until they have passed being your responsibility. You will remain concerned for a long time about how your children are bringing together sexual and loving feelings; and if they are able to enjoy a sexual relationship which is satisfying to them and does not leave them feeling isolated. Beware your attempted solutions, precipitating action rather than constraining it.

We think that most parents have at some time the wish that their children will have less pain than they have had, less serious physical illnesses, and less fear of their parents than they themselves had. Parents will wish their children to have had better opportunities at school. They will wish the world to be a better place for them. Do you also wish that your children will have better sex lives than you?

Sex and Contraception

To recognise that you are able to become grandparents is the step that you have to take when facing your children's sexuality.

The general view of society today seems to be that adolescents should have a great deal of information about reproduction, the sex act and contraception. Society also has laws about the age at which people can indulge in sex: forbidding sex for girls under the age of 16 was an attempt to inhibit child prostitution. Society encourages sexual activity only inside relationships such as marriage. And there is discouragement of early commitment to such a relationship, lest people make choices which are difficult for them to live with.

On the whole, we have no quarrel with this way of seeing things. Simply, we wish to try to present something which may be of help for parents, coping with their grandparenthood, and adolescents with their sexuality for the first time. But we have no answers.

People do not talk about sex. They make jokes about it, allude to it or avoid it. Not talking about sex differs in quality from not talking about your bowels or your bladder or your income.

Sex is enjoyed.

Sex makes babies.

Sex may be part of relationships, of bonding, and is certainly part of reproduction.

Sex is used in advertising and society pressures people to conform to certain sexual norms or stereotypes.

Pregnancy and Marriage

We have talked already about sex and contraception, the dilemma that parents face between not condoning early sexual activity for their children on the one hand and, on the other, wanting them to take precautions so that they do not get pregnant sooner than they are ready. We have talked about it. You have to decide, making the decision based on what you are most anxious about. Whatever decision you make we may call the best decision.

In fact, you are worried about pregnancy. No matter how well intentioned and how well thought out your relationship is with your adolescent in this area, there are some whose children actually do start the process of creating a new life. For the parents of a girl who becomes pregnant there is far more impact and consequence than if you are the parents of a boy who impregnates a girl. What can you do about it?

1. Throw her out in the snow and tell her never to darken your doorstep again.
2. Ignore it and hope it will go away. After all it is a temporary condition and will end. She may after all be only slightly pregnant, like a dose of flu.
3. Counsel abortion.
4. Offer to adopt the child as your own.
5. Make a room available in the house for the new mother and child.
6. Apply for admission to a private mother and baby home.
7. Refer the case to social services and tell them to deal with it.
8. Start making plans for an early wedding.
9. Enquire about arrangements for adoption.

We are not going to tell you what to do. Just as we advise not telling your son or daughter what to do. What we do say is, try to be as clear as possible about what your response is and what you are prepared to offer. It is going to be a disruption. How much disruption can you stand?

If the course is abortion, we do recommend that this is not taken lightly. By this we do not mean that we are arguing against abortion, but simply that we strongly believe that a girl having an abortion, or a natural spontaneous miscarriage, will make use of counselling and support. However much that pregnancy may not have been wanted, loss of pregnancy or loss of that child is a loss which may have reverberations for a long time, and for children not yet conceived.

At its simplest, just think of the relationship which you have with your daughter now compared with that which your mother had with you at the same age. What sort of anxieties did your own mother have about your sexuality? What controls did she try to place upon you? Did she worry about your getting pregnant? How would she, or did she, handle it? Did she worry about your getting pregnant more or less than you worried about getting pregnant? Do you think that you worry more or less about your daughter's getting pregnant than you think she does herself? Or, if worry is too strong a word, do you think that you *think* about the possibility of your daughter's getting pregnant more or less than you think she *thinks* about it herself?

Amy in March

> Amy always felt sad in March because March was the time of the year that her baby would have been born if she had not had the abortion. But she said it was better to feel that than to face what she thinks she would have had to face if that baby, conceived so unlovingly, had been born. She went on feeling her March sadness throughout her marriage and the joy of bringing up of her own children. The regrets were something that she could not get away from, but she still felt that she had made the best decision.
>
> She sometimes wondered what would have happened if she had later not been able to have children and how she would have felt then. To this she found no answer.

The priest in a Graham Greene novel, Monsignor Quixote, says 'One can't escape regrets.'

Parental Sexuality

One of the things that children have difficulty in appreciating is that you parents have any active sexual life at all. It may not be that they cannot see you being that sort of person; they just do not think about it. It is not in their frame of reference, perhaps partly because you seem so old.

One of the things that might confront this non-interest of theirs is if one of you has taken on a new partner. This is a confrontation of the most blatant kind that proves you are somebody who has an active sex life. For instance: when a single mother lets a man sleep in her bed, when a widowed father has girlfriends who stay the night, or when a new friend goes on holiday with the family and stays in the parental room.

You do not have to ask your children's permission to resume a sex life with a new adult; but if you take a new partner, you might ask them how they feel about it.

9

Drugs

For comment on drugs, we turn to a pupil's sociological essay:

Some Methods of Destruction Used by a Community
This report summarises our findings on just one aspect of the intricate, highly organised society which we studied – its use of drugs.

Drug A was advertised and sold openly, and dispensed in places of refreshment. Its use was ritualised in industry where workforce and management had negotiated times for breaks for its taking. No written age restriction operated and while, for all the drugs which we observed taken in this society, social pressure was strongest for A, it did seem to be unusual for it to be offered before puberty.

Drug B was available in licensed dispensaries and from other sales premises, both of which displayed advertisements and certification by the authorities. There were written instructions forbidding the sale to inhabitants under the age of 18, but in private dwellings and on common land consumption was permitted. There was some attempt to measure body levels of B in the populace and to restrict the use of certain mechanical equipment to those keeping below that level. For the licence, merchants paid a fee to the authorities who also reaped a heavy tax from each sale. In return, it seemed, the authorities helped maintain the merchants' monopoly by coming down heavily on pedlars of D and E.

Drug C was also sold in many places where again licensing was the rule and was displayed. There were penalties for selling, but not giving, C to those under 16, but this issue was dealt with by the use of automatic, unmanned kiosks which dispensed the drug on the insertion of a readily available counter. As in the case of B, the majority of the cost borne by the taker was passed directly to the authorities in a special tax. Some restrictions in public places on account of the smell.

Drug D was limited to a far smaller proportion of the population, mostly younger people who often used it in conjunction with C. There were no licences for this drug which was declared illegal, leading to a flourishing 'black market'. Smugglers and sales people risked heavy fines or imprisonent, and to this end were pursued by squads hired by the authorities largely financed on the proceeds of the taxes on B and C.

Drug E appeared to be more of a minority taste and was more expensive. It was used in various levels of purity or contamination. Again this substance was banned and, if anything, we noticed that the hired squads showed more enthusiasm for capturing this than D.

Substance F was curious. It seems that it had been widely available in the society for many years but that only relatively recently had its mind-affecting properties (when inhaled) been detected. It seemed to us that in some almost paradoxical way its very availability and the simple shift of use from domestic commodity to drug, pre-occupied the consumers of A, B and C and the authorities, dependent on the taxes on B and C.

Litter from B and C was frequently to be seen in the street or after public gatherings.

The effects of these drugs

Drug A is a stimulant and increases the secretion of urine. New users or people who suddenly increase their dose, may experience restlessness. Some of our observers thought that there was a connection between the widespread use of this stimulant and the widespread dispensing in institutions and by some caring professions of sedative antidotes. Others of our team were of a different opinion and thought the two were not linked.

Drug B had a depressant action and some inhibition of the sense of pain. We thought that it was the second most addictive substance in the society and we noticed many organisations for the care of those so addicted. A particular characteristic of its addiction was the requirement of an increasing dose and neglect of adequate diet.

Drug C was peculiar in that the new user experienced predominantly unpleasant effects, nausea and coughing, while the regular user did not. It did have a certain tranquillising effect and we think research may show influence on nerve endings; but its main effect for the user was the very simple one that each dose dealt with the desire for that dose. It was by far the most addictive of all the substances we studied.

Drug D had the effect of lightening the mental state and we thought there was good evidence that people using it would be less able to handle complex machinery with safety. Many users reported feelings of warmth and goodwill.

Drug E was also reported to be a mind lightener and to give the taker a temporary feeling of peace. This substance was also as addictive as B, but while some people, as with C, were able to maintain an absolutely steady dose for many years, this was difficult for others because of the various concentrations in which it was available.

F gave very rapid alteration of mood and often near loss of consciousness.

Dangers

All the drugs were potentially dangerous:

A leads to chronic irritability.

B causes more inability to work and disruption of close emotional relationships than any other.

C causes more ill-health and premature death than any of the others and, in so doing, causes disruption of families and loss of industrial capacity.

D's chief dangers appear to occur if the subject attempts complex mechanical tasks while intoxicated, and simply through some of the things that happen when people break laws.

E, for some who were rich or skilled enough to obtain pure supplies, appeared relatively safe, so long as no complicated mechanical tasks were attempted. However, most supplies were so contaminated that they were dangerous and the criminal element so strong that the drug had wide social implications.

F required skilled use. Most users were not skilled; they suffered facial burns, brain damage or death.

We found ourselves bemused by a multitude of names used for all these substances and there was even copyright on some of them. We give just one, which seemed in each case universally understood:

A caffeine, B alcohol, C tobacco, D marijuana, E heroin, F glue or solvent.

Parents

We have introduced the subject in this way not because we do not take the subject seriously, but because we want to stimulate thinking into trying to find creative solutions to problems that we know worry you greatly. We do not under-estimate your anxiety and your worry, particularly in a climate when there appears to be growing use of some drugs, but we do want to redress some of the imbalance in the way that dangers in the use of drugs are pointed out.

When people talk or write about drugs they usually mean the 'hard', narcotic drugs like heroin or 'soft' illegal ones like marijuana. We think there are also real dangers from the use of drugs that are socially acceptable, such as tobacco and alcohol. (Note that our pupil essayist let off one section of the population that has several times in the last two decades been billed as the largest group of addicts – namely middle-aged women on minor tranquillisers and sleeping pills.) The dangers are even greater because adults condone or deny their use. One of the significant messages that young people are given by our culture is that to be adult is synonymous with smoking and drinking alcohol. That is, with taking drugs.

Stages of Anxiety

There are probably several stages that all parents go through when they are concerned or anxious about their children's taking drugs. We recognise that parents can be anxious about their children's taking drugs, even if their children are not taking drugs. One can be anxious about things that are not happening. Many parents may say 'Well, we just do not know. Our children do not tell us anything so how can we be sure?' You cannot be absolutely sure, but there are ways of allaying or reinforcing your suspicions.

Recognition

First, do you have any real evidence that things have changed? Remember the general context of a great deal of changes in your child and in the relationship between you and your child. The physical changes alone can contribute to changes in mood, irritability, etc. But some of the more well-known drugs do have particular signs associated with their use. Some drugs affect the size of the pupils of the eyes.

Tobacco

Forgive us if we start once again with tobacco. You can smell this on clothing, both from someone's smoking or from his being in the presence of others who have been smoking. Your best opportunity to get him to stop might be by making a fuss when you first notice this. At the early stage your children will probably be most anxious about your finding out and your doing anything about it. Therefore it is the time of greatest influence. Remember how we have said 'rules' start. Do not let drug experimentation be associated with the rule 'parents say nothing about it'. People starting to smoke may cough, suffer loss of appetite and have stained fingers.

Alcohol

Like tobacco, this makes the breath smell. Dinner money can be spent on alcohol. Find out from them what they ate while at school. If boys or girls return from a party in a particularly excited and flushed state, this might reinforce your suspicions. You could question more closely about what actually happened at the party, but do remember to think of a way that will give you maximum information rather than maximum resistance.

Marijuana

People who smoke marijuana almost certainly started by smoking cigarettes first. The link between marijuana and harder drugs, such as heroin, is often made. We have not seen this link between tobacco and heroin emphasised as much. Marijuana takers may appear euphoric. They may not be able to think very coherently or be able to give clear words to their thoughts.

Heroin

Heroin is mostly taken by injection and this leaves marks. It has become more common for young people to start by smoking it, in the mistaken view that this way does not lead to addiction. It does, and the next step, injection, is very, very close. Be suspicious if your child is suddenly anxious about covering up arms or does not want to appear in swimming gear.

Solvent abuse

Most commonly this is glue-sniffing, but adolescents have been known to inhale a whole variety of substances, some of them extremely dangerous and which may lead to death very quickly. Solvents cause sore mouths, lips and nose and the mental effects are very much like drunkenness.

Pills

There are many different pills that can be taken: some are

stimulants and some are sedatives. They all alter mood but do so without causing the breath to smell.

Actions for Parents

What can you do about it? Of the whole range of things you could do, there are some to which we might encourage you more than others. Never underestimate the power of going to the police if you think your child has been involved in doing something illegal. We know the great difficulty this causes parents and the accusation that might be thrown at them that they are 'shopping' their children. You must decide which difficulty you find easier to live with.

You can apply sanctions. While we are not suggesting that you lock up your daughters and sons in their rooms, we do want to point out that you can cause consequences: you can curtail their free time, insist they stay within the home for certain hours, make sure you always know where they are, have them constantly supervised, reduce their financial allowances. You know your children best and are better able to judge what will influence them, and what things you can bear to do.

There are solutions to do with talking. And there are many different ways of talking to your children about things like these. You can threaten them, plead with them, offer to bribe them: you can do nothing at all. You can make a very clear statement of what your position is, that you will not tolerate its happening and you will not support it in any way, but at the same time you will be sympathetic and try very hard to understand. It is possible not to condone actions but, at the same time, to try to understand the reasons for them.

You may, for instance, make it quite clear that you reserve the right to search an adolescent's room when you are very anxious, because that is a way that you feel you have to deal with your anxiety. You must once again balance your views on privacy and rights against your anxiety about your child's general well-being and health. We do wish to emphasise that if you say or do any of these things, you do so quite explicitly under what we call the 'frame' of your own anxiety. There is little more provocative for adolescents than to be told that something is being done for their own good. Far better, in our view, to say 'I am doing this because of my anxiety' . . . 'I am so worried about X that I have decided' . . . We think that adolescents are better able to appreciate your caring for them if you appear more direct about your own distress which is driving you to behave as you are.

You may think that we are not telling you what to do clearly enough and that you would prefer us to give you a more straightforward answer. We cannot give an answer which would apply to each case, but in general encourage you to act positively rather than negatively; to decide what you are going to do, rather than what you are not going to do.

The hardest thing to do may be to look at what part you have played in your child's behaviour. You will gather that one of our themes in this book is to abandon ideas to do with blame but rather to look at how, in a family, each member's behaviour has an effect and in part determines or maintains the behaviour of everyone else. So a more useful question you might ask yourself is, 'What am I doing to keep it going?' There are also organisations and publications, such as some of those listed at the end of this book, that you might be able to use.

Adolescents

And now we want to try to talk to you adolescents. Right away let us acknowledge that nearly everyone that we know seems to have had a drink in a pub before legal age. The laws to do with drugs are among the most widely flouted in our society.

If you found a newly-discovered community of human

beings, who had no mind-altering drugs at all, would you introduce alcohol to them?

We know the messages adults give about drugs are often confusing. Even though we know that the use of some drugs is, to some extent, socially acceptable, we still advocate that their use be limited. This is because we have some anxieties about them which we should like to share with you.

We find it difficult to compete with our cautionary tales against all the excitement that goes with taking drugs. There is something instant, commanding and dramatic about the effects of taking the mind-altering drugs. There are few things that are so different, that create such a sense of difference. We acknowledge this. In the course of watching television programmes, we have noted with interest the views of certain groups of people who have had exhilarating feelings when falling from high places. Stuntmen have talked about the excitement of falling from a high building, the wind on their faces, the sensation of the ground rushing up to meet them. In all stunts of this sort there is usually a soft substance that will break the stuntman's fall. There are people in Polynesia who jump from high platforms with ropes tied round their ankles, so that they stop centimetres from the ground. They, when interviewed, have talked about the sacred and religious experiences of their act and the way that their consciousness has been altered while taking part in it. Mexicans who dive from the high cliffs in Acapulco for the benefit of the tourists have spoken of the religious significance of their act. In fact they have a brief period of worship at an altar before they dive. They have described the exhilaration of diving at the right time into the water below, and missing the rocks. There is the circus stunt act of diving into a very small tank of water.

In all these acts, no matter how exhilarating, exciting and different or religious the fall or dive may be, there is something there at the end that usually breaks the fall.

We can only liken drugs to making those jumps without

knowing that any of those things will be there to break the fall. If there is not, one has to hope that the concrete will be soft enough. When you take drugs, because of the other things associated with them, the sub-cultures, the gangs, the crime links, the chemical impurities, the lessened supervision or security because of the very illegality of it – there may be nothing but concrete at the bottom.

It may sound very precious to say so and, at the risk of sounding like your parents, we do say that we are really worried about your getting into bad company. If you are taking drugs, list what you get from them, then try to find out if there are any other ways in which you can achieve those same things.

Altered States – Getting High

One of the things on your list may be what we call altered states of consciousness – getting high. There are other ways of achieving this. Meditating, relaxation, yoga, music, or certain physical activity, may have similar effects. There are now some very good books available about altered states and self-hypnosis. These seem pretty safe activities to us.

Try reading this exercise, as if you were telling someone else what to do, into a tape recorder. Then play it back and follow your instructions.

Sit comfortably so that if you do not move you will not get pins and needles.

Let your eyes rest on something ahead of you and take note of three things that you can see in your outer field of vision. Let yourself hear three things and let them be noises from as far away as possible (can you hear the wind, can you hear traffic, can you hear birds, can you hear people talking in the next street and noises in other parts of the building?) Let yourself be aware of three parts of your body: say your left foot, your right shoulder and your left ear.

Now let yourself notice just two things in your field of vision.

Let yourself notice two noises near to you; maybe this time it has to be one of the noises that you are making yourself. Let yourself be aware of two parts of your body: the sole of one of your feet and where the skin of two of your fingers touch.

Now do the same, but only one thing. First, look at your eyebrows, or as near to them as you can get. Second, listen to the sound of your own breathing. Third, think of your own heart beating and perhaps you may be aware of the sensation.

As you look up at your eyebrows, take a deep breath. Then very slowly let your breath out as you let your upper lids close, while all the time keeping your eyes looking up.

Now let your eyeballs lower to a comfortable position.

Now let yourself be aware of different parts of your body in turn: first your toes, then your ankles, then your calves, then your knees, and so on.

Let yourself count silently; each time you breathe out, starting at ten and going down to one.

If you want to do something more, you may just repeat in your own mind the word 'one'.

Let the tape run on silently for five minutes. Then record into it again:

Now let yourself count from one to ten and then feel free to open your eyes.

In doing this, let as many thoughts as come, come and go. We call it letting go.

You can experiment with your own variations.

Society is as it is. Even if some of the substances in certain drugs may not be particularly physically harmful, we are concerned about the culture that surrounds their use and distribution. It just is so difficult to be involved in one part and not the other.

Mark did not know

Mark's school work was deteriorating and he was dropped from the football team. He was faced with choices about what he wanted in his life. He felt that the world was not arranged as it should have been. Over the previous year he had been taking more drugs. He had started off with the occasional pill at the disco, then marijuana, and now his taking of amphetamines was quite regular.

After school open-day his parents confronted him about his poor showing at school. 'Maybe you should go and see your doctor – are you not well? Do you need a tonic or a pick-me-up?'

He said to his friend that he had been treated unfairly by being thrown off the football team: 'It was me that scored the two goals that won the cup last year'.

But his friend said, 'Well, it's not going to be you that scores the two goals that win the cup this year, is it?' They had a big argument over this and Mark got angry with his friend.

That night at the disco, the person who usually sold him drugs approached him with, 'Want a pick-me-up now, Mark?'

Mark replied, 'Not this evening'.

One of the thoughts that was going through Mark's mind was that the drugs had become more important than everything else. The decision he was faced with was, 'Do I want to stay like that or not?' He decided that he just did not know but would have to make a decision soon before his chances dried up.

Human beings seem always to have been interested in altering their environment and their mental state. Historically they seem first to have done this without drugs but for a few thousand years to have used drugs of one sort or another. The most common are tobacco, alcohol and caffeine.

Tobacco

Tobacco is the most addictive substance ever known to human beings. If cigarette smoke is inhaled, nicotine is in the brain faster than heroin arrives there if injected into a vein. We say that tobacco is dangerous even though we are sure that is well known to you. However if you do smoke and want not do, we do suggest that you remember that this is a piece of voluntary behaviour and again we remind you that it is erroneous to assume that actions necessarily follow feelings. Just because you feel like a cigarette does not mean that you have (a) to buy or accept a cigarette (b) to hold a cigarette (c) to put a cigarette in your mouth (d) to set light to it.

We try to be neutral about most things, but other people's smoking has tested us to the limit and we have given up our neutrality. We have felt persecuted, pained, discomfited, angered and frustrated by people who smoke in our presence. We just do not like it. If any of you who are reading our book smoke and are dropping ash on the pages, stop doing it, because we don't like to think of it. If you are worried about your parents' smoking and do not want them to do it, you have our full support. We sympathise with you. But how you are going to get them to stop is, of course, another matter altogether.

Alcohol

Alcohol is much less dangerous but can make you feel sick, make you feel that you have got no energy, so you do not bother to eat food well, and can reduce your inhibitions against behaviours normally foreign to you. In more than small quantities it can damage the only liver you have got and it is easy to depend on it. Like so many things in life it can be a pleasure that you pay for.

Marijuana

Marijuana is, in our view, probably less dangerous physiologically than either of the above two; but it is illegal. Therefore we recommend that you do not take marijuana.

We add the obvious warning, that through its illegality, you may be introduced to the hard drugs which we know are dangerous. You will know that many people are making money from the distribution of hard drugs to young people.

Heroin

This is the most exciting drug because it gets the most media attention. You will have seen TV programmes about drug pushers and intrepid policemen who thwart them. It can give you an incredibly ecstatic feeling the first time you take it, but then, very soon, you get into taking it to stop feeling awful. The need to stop feeling like this is so great and the drug so expensive, that users are prepared to go to any lengths, regardless of risks to their personal health, personal relationships and personal liberty. Taken in any way, it is just as dangerous. Those who decide that they want to stop are incredibly difficult to help.

Glue-sniffing

Solvents are quite legal, fairly expensive, messy, and can be dangerous. They provide a nasty way to deteriorate and, as we said earlier, mental states can be altered pretty well by other means which can give you a lot of fun.

Pills

We think people, especially of your parents' generation, take too many pills, and most of them unnecessarily. They are often associated with medicine which is always thought to be good for you. (We have written about the dangers of treatments, doctors and hospitals in some of our other work.) Pills are easy to pass around and are therefore very tempting. They may make you feel very up or very down and may be called almost just that. They affect your perception, your thinking, your co-ordination; like other chemicals, they can damage your body.

Our Message

We have not attempted to classify or comment on every type of drug that may be used. This subject is dealt with comprehensively in many places and if you want more facts, you can get them. We hope you have been able to pick up our two themes in this chapter: to you adolescents, not to start and if you have, then to stop; to you parents, act positively and look closely at how you might be doing something, however small, that helps to keep it going.

10

Family Break-up

Separation

Nothing brings out parents' humanity quite so much as when their marriages break up. Their clay feet are really seen then. Here was something which they could not maintain.

Each one of you will know someone whose parents have split up even if yours themselves have not done so yet. We say yet, because they are going to split up when one of them dies. You may be interested to know that in the centuries preceding this one, marriages lasted for no longer on average than now. These days it is divorce that ends marriages; then it was death.

However modern a couple may be when they set up together, we think that they will, at least for a moment, have the idea that their relationship might go on for ever. We think that, however modern parents are, if they are living together when the children are born, they will give those children, one way or another, the impression that their relationship will be everlasting.

By the time your parents make the final decision to separate, you and they will have had some time to get used to the idea that they are not going to be together for ever. They are likely to be further along the line of acceptance than you are, however, but may expect you to join them simultaneously at the same point on that line. Their guilt about their relationship not having lasted, or about their parenting of you not having been as stable or as perfect as they had wished, may lead them sometimes to be angry with you for some of the things that you do.

Certain children may feel that some of these things are their fault. Even if they do not feel so, it is difficult for somebody who has been brought up by two parents, when they split, not to feel or to dream or to wonder if it might not be something 'to do with me'. But, of course, if you have read this book so far, we hope that you will be sharing with us the conviction that nothing is so simple as the fault lying with just one person. We call it viewing relationships as a system.

But, anyway, it is the parents' job to manage their own relationship. Whether it lasts or does not, we certainly think that how well or badly they manage this will affect you.

We expect that you, their adolescent child, will find it quite hard to know what is your business and what is not. Just as they affect you, you too can affect them. We expect that your parents are not making a perfect job of ending their present relationship and negotiating a new one. This will present you with some difficulty in how you relate to them. They may find it hard to give you as clear messages as they used to. They may try to draw you into their confidence or to take their side. Other members of the family network (your grandparents, for example) may further complicate things by giving you their views or asking for yours.

And it might take them some time to get used to the idea that no matter what happens your mother and father will always share one relationship. That is as your parents.

How can you get through this?

If it is your own parents who split up, you will, of course, feel quite different from when it happens to your friends' parents. It is one of the most startling life events you will ever remember facing. Your parents change from being a couple to being separate people. One of them prefers to be somewhere else than to continue living at home with you. You know that one of them has chosen to leave you rather than stay with you. However much you feel drawn to the one that leaves, there is no escaping the fact that that is what is happening. If one of them is leaving to live with someone else, you will be getting as big a confrontation with their sex life as you are ever likely to encounter. It is not suprising if you find all this very difficult.

Here you are at the time of your own sexual experimentation and you are probably quite preoccupied with it. You will have seen or received messages about sexual morality and the accepted ways of conducting your own sex life so that when your parents publicly disclose a change in theirs, you may feel many things.

Gary and his parents' separation

Gary hated it. He felt angry with both of them. He had been really enjoying his own life and he found it very interesting. His friends, football, some of the subjects he was doing at school and his bike, were the things that took up most of his time. He had had a girlfriend for a few weeks. His new awareness of girls, and their shapes, was very exciting.

Suddenly his father was leaving home. One evening his parents had brought him and his brother together and told them that they were splitting up. He had always known that parents were funny people, that his mum and dad rowed, had peculiar ideas on a whole number of topics and had tastes in music and newspapers which he could not abide. But here was something of an utterly different dimension, something which he could not ignore.

Gary talked it over with his friend Grant whose parents had split up two years before. Grant said that when it happened to him he had sat down and worked out what was his business and what was not. He had made a list.

My business
1. Where am I going to live?
2. What effect will it have on my chances of going to a university or getting a steady girlfriend?
3. How much money shall we have?

4. Will it be more expensive for my parents living apart so that they will have less money for me?
5. Shall I still be able to go on the ski holiday with school?
6. Which one is going to leave and which one will stay and how much will I see of the one that leaves?
7. Will my brother and me be split up?
8. Shall I have to take sides, and, if so, whose side?

Not my business

1. What my parents do with their own lives.
2. Why they split up.

Then Grant said to Gary that although making the list had helped a bit, he was still left with some nasty questions. Was it his fault? After all, his father had often said to him that things were his fault and his mother had often said to him that he was putting a strain on his father. But he had decided that was crazy. Parents who separate do not separate because of their children but for their own reasons.

After a few days Gary felt he could begin to tackle it.

James and his 'dad'

James had been 11 and his sister Teresa 14 when his Italian father and English mother split up. His father went back to Italy while James remained in England with his mother and sister. His great hobby was fishing, something that his father had often promised to join in with him but never had done. Every Saturday he would browse through the latest fishing magazines in his local angling shop, looking at expensive rods, fishing tackle and bait. The owner of the shop, Jeremy, became quite friendly with James and they would talk at length about the latest equipment.

One day James brought his mother to the shop with him to see the expensive fishing rod that he particularly coveted for his Christmas present. His mother, Mary, and the shop owner got on like a house on fire. Jeremy started calling at the house and started going out with Mary. A year later they were married and James was delighted. His sister was not as pleased as he was, but was not particularly displeased either.

After James's 14th birthday things started to become more

difficult at home. The usual adolescent behaviour of untidy rooms and not looking after the fabric of the house became the topics of constant rows between James and his mother. Jeremy would intervene and at times talk at length to James about his difficult behaviour. Of course they would still often go out fishing, but then James stopped. His fishing tackle, expanded since Jeremy had come into the house, lay unused. He started being rude and surly and shouting at Jeremy as well.

The pattern soon became established. Mary would moan at James about not doing his school work or keeping his room tidy; Jeremy would intervene and start telling James what he should do, and telling him to listen to his mother more. James would get into a row with Jeremy and walk straight out of the house or into his bedroom. The next day, or the day after, the battle would continue. Jeremy did not know what to do.

In desperation Mary wrote to her ex-husband in Italy to see if he would take James. She got a letter back that her ex-husband was not in a position to do so. One day in the middle of a blazing row James shouted at Jeremy, 'I don't know why you keep interfering in all this, you are not my dad, just my mother's bloody husband.' Jeremy was very hurt and angry at this remark because, even before his entry into the family, he felt that he had tried to be a father to James.

In bed that night, Jeremy and Mary talked about the incident and Jeremy shared his hurt and anger over what James had said. 'You know, love,' said Mary, 'he may be right. Not the way he said it to you but what he was saying. You have enough on your plate just being my husband and married to me; maybe all that you should do is try to support me because I have the job of being both parents to him. We must sort something out. It is not that I do not appreciate your support because I do need it a lot.'

The next day at breakfast, Jeremy said to James, 'Look, about yesterday, what you said about me not being your dad.'

'Oh, forget it,' said James, 'I was angry.'

'No, you are right,' said Jeremy. 'I am not your dad, I am your mum's husband and I want to concentrate on that in future and to support her. But know I am always around and I am here.'

'Okay,' said James, stopping himself just in time from calling Jeremy, 'Dad'.

Patrick's new wife

Patrick was appalled when his marriage ended and his wife apparently crazily disappeared leaving him to look after their two children. He managed all right, or at any rate not too badly; and they survived as a threesome but he did feel persecuted by it. He bemoaned this new experience, which so many of his generation seemed to be having. He had become a single parent and wondered how he could ever make the transition to a new relationship. His own parents had had a stable marriage and he felt that his generation was quite unprepared for this new experiment in living. He felt a sort of martyred pioneer.

Then on an Easter holiday he took his children on a walk round a country churchyard and they all started reading the inscriptions. He suddenly realised that years before, hundreds and hundreds of people had died in young middle age leaving their spouses behind. He felt an immense and surprising sense of companionship with and affinity for his Victorian forebears who had been bringing up children without a spouse. He then remembered that his own grandmother had done just that after losing her husband in the First World War. She had later remarried.

It was some months after this revelation that he felt more peaceful in himself and started to go out. He met Tracey and started a new relationship. She seemed to be accepted well enough by his children and they did not raise any objections when she joined the household or even when she and their father announced that they would marry.

Tracey was, however, very nervous. The kernel of her worry, which she managed to share with Patrick in bed one night, was how she could possibly be a mother of children of 12 and 14, who had been produced, brought up and abandoned by another woman. How could she possibly be a stepmother? In some ways she felt that being called a stepmother was worse than being called a spinster. 'We all know,' she said, 'the Cinderella story. 'I don't want to be seen as the wicked stepmother. I just dread that image.'

'Hey, wait a minute,' said Patrick. 'I don't see you as a

stepmother at all. The proposal that I made to you is that we marry. And we stay here, you as my wife and I as your husband. The children, much as I love them, are an extra to our relationship. With my support I hope that you and they will work out a relationship which will be satisfactory to both sides and to me, and I hope that you will support me in being a father to them. Please see yourself as my wife, not as coming here as their stepmother. Let us do one thing at a time.'

11

Health and Medicine

Do you realise that your body is you? We start by asking this question, knowing that you may think it is silly, because we think that however liberally, progressively, understandingly, you may be brought up it is quite difficult to realise, when you are alone and unexposed to social restraints, that your body really is yours, to touch, to look at, anywhere or anyhow you like. Many people seem to experience more hesitation in doing this than in, say, turning on a favourite piece of music.

But, of course, parents, that body used to be your responsibility. You had to hold it and feed it, wash it, keep it warm. When did you stop having to do those things or feel that you should? When did you stop feeling a sense of responsibility for its very continued existence? Do you remember when you last wiped your son' or daughter's bottom, when you last dressed him or her? Do you still decide when their sheets should be changed, when their ears are cleaned or their teeth should be brushed? Do you still make the appointments for the dentist?

The area of consent to medical treatment for your children has become a focus of controversy. We have felt that 16 was a useful cut-off point for decisions about medical treatment to be transferred from parents to young people. The law changes in other areas in respect of what people of 16 can or cannot do, and for what they can or cannot be held accountable.

Current debate in our society over this issue is highlighted by the controversy over contraception advice and prescription for girls under 16. One view is that the doctor/patient relationship should be as confidential as the adolescent girl wants it to be. It is not clear whether those who take this view do so on moral and philosophical grounds, or on the practical wish to limit the number of unwanted pregnancies. Another view is that no treatment should take place without parental consent because they are the ones who are responsible. We do not know whether the general practitioner with this view will treat the 15-year-old boy with gonorrhea without his parents' consent.

Letter from a Parent to a Doctor

Dear Dr Lambert,
I am sure you have been following with interest the recent court case to do with contraceptive advice for girls under the age of 16. I feel my daughter, Sandie, who is now 14, would come to you for such advice more readily if she knew that she had control over the sharing of this information with me.

If she were to come to you without telling me – which I hope does not happen – I give my consent for you to advise and prescribe to Sandie as you see fit, without telling me.

Sandie knows that I am writing to you along these lines.
Yours sincerely,
Martha Rogers.

After Sandie's mother had shown her the letter, she said to her, 'But you do know what I want for you, don't you? I really don't want you to start having sex too soon.'

We do not put forward any moral view of what is right or wrong behaviour. We do say that we have found it more useful for there to be an acknowledged cut-off point for the transfer of responsibility from parents to the adolescent.

Whatever the law and the legal position are when you are reading this, we hope that you go to a doctor who will encourage you to share things with your parents, but do not be surprised if you find some doctors and some clinics clearer on this issue than others.

Once you decide to have a professional relationship with your doctor, the question of who is in charge comes up. Doctors do not have to see you. They decide, in the first instance, who goes on their list and who does not. Once they do decide to see you and you to consult them, do remember that what doctors say to you is not a command or orders. It is advice, but they sometimes forget this. Sometimes, if they are not clear themselves what advice they can best give you, they might refer you to somebody else who is a specialist, for a second opinion. This person, even though a specialist, still has only advice to offer you. What we are saying, of course, is very difficult to put into practice because even sceptics like we are very often take what doctors say to us as gospel. It is very difficult to decide not to do what they suggest or even to question it. Very often, people's worries about health are such that they want an expert to tell them what to do before they can start feeling better. At these times they ignore the evidence that doctors, too, are fallible, out of a wish to have somebody who knows what is best.

Please remember that a lot of medicine is a grey area in which there are no clear answers but only possible avenues of exploration. Remember that most physical complaints limit themselves without recourse to drugs or doctoring. They just go away.

How to Help Yourselves

There are many ways of changing what you feel by yourself. This might be about a concern with something that is happening with your body, whether it be a sense of well-being or anything else. For instance, you can do something about your spots. Touching them helps them to grow. A particular cleansing agent may help them to go away. Keen as we are on paying attention to what we eat, in this area of spots eating does not seem to have any significance.

You may feel much better about your spots, however, when you see a pop star, or one of your friends, who has them as well.

We do encourage you to pay heed to what you eat. Just imagine all the things that you take in during the day. Remember that whatever you have taken in is going to become part of you. Parents also please note that what you are feeding your children is what they are going to become.

We hope you have looked at yourself in the mirror (and that you have one in your room). We should like you to have the same sense of 'that is me' when you look at the food you are going to eat.

In our chapter on drugs (9) we have written about other ways of changing how you feel than by the more well-known things like tobacco, alcohol, marijuana, hard drugs and glue. You can experiment with your breathing, try relaxation, self-hypnosis, massage, meditation or just deciding to feel well or better. You may have a feeling in your head that you decide to give the label of migraine. We think similar feelings in the head have probably happened to people long before anyone decided to call them migraine. We should like you to experiment by not giving that feeling a label. Instead, just acknowledge that you are feeling something and then try to change it to feeling differently.

Pain is an emotional experience and, as such, can be modified. While drugs are a way of modifying this, which many people find useful, we do wish to draw to your attention the possibility of doing something about it yourself. The sort of exercise we have given for altering your mental state is used by some women several times a day before their period starts, and during the time when they usually get the pain. They say it makes a difference.

> Focus your attention on wherever in your body you get pain; in
> your imagination see the power of your own blood cells and let
> them calm, soothe, and absorb the pain. Let the blood cells, and
> the pain, have an imaginary shape and form. You may have
> seen the computer game with the little figure eating up spiders.

When you are in pain you hold your body in a particular way.
This affects the way you breathe. Try changing the way you
breathe so that your body becomes more relaxed. This, in
turn, may make bearing the pain easier. At the same time,
you may imagine each breath, as you lengthen and slow it, as
a force that will calm your pain.

Admission to Hospital

One of your family will be admitted to hospital and we
reckon it is more likely to be one of the adults, simply
because they have been going for longer and are more likely
to break down or need repair like any piece of older machinery
does. It may be that your mother goes into hospital for the
delivery of a new brother or sister for you, a jolt for the
system in all senses of the word and a shaking reminder to
you of your parents' continuing sexuality. It may be for
investigation or treatment of a more serious thing with
consequences even more far reaching.

But life goes on while somebody is in hospital. The admitted
person may wonder about 're-entry', and the people at home
may have considerable conflicts about how much attention
and energy they put into their life at home and how much
into visiting whoever it is in hospital.

In any one National Health Service district of about a
couple of hundred thousand people, there would be about 20
adolescents in hospital at any time. They have appendicitis,
broken legs, motor-bike accidents, burns, leukemia, plastic
surgery, etc. Who decided they should be there? This is an
issue of where people live. Our view is that until you are 16,

your parents decide where you live. Over the next two years you negotiate between your parents and yourselves and after 18 it is entirely up to you so long as you have the co-operation of landlords.

In the field of psychiatry there are special wards for adolescents. We have worked a lot with some of them. We do not think the notion that some people are crazy and some people are not is helpful, and we have come to the conclusion that it is not how crazily people have been acting, or how sick they are, that determines whether they go into hospital or not, but simply whether they can be coped with by those who are in charge of or around them.

Parents and adolescents, if you do have any dealings with psychiatrists, do make sure that you get them to explain what they mean in a way which you understand. They will not mind doing this for you, and, indeed, they may feel quite flattered.

If you go into a general hospital, however, you are unlikely to be living in one of those few parts of the country where there is a special adolescent ward in a general hospital. You are likely therefore, as an adolescent, to end up with younger children or with the very old. Nobody really knows what this is like except those adolescents who have had the experience and, as far as we know, their reminiscences have not been collected. There will have been some things they have liked and some things they have disliked. That goes for the staff too. Some of the questions that adolescents have brought to our notice are: how to masturbate if both arms are in plaster; how to deal with the tickle of sticking plaster or plaster-of-Paris; is it bad manners to laugh about teenage jokes when other people around are dying?

It may be more difficult for an adolescent to deal with the idea that life is still going on outside, than for parents to remember it. It is as if you are living in suspension. Will you be able to pick up things easily afterwards? Will the outside be changed? Will your boyfriend have gone out with somebody else or will you have changed what you feel about him? Will you be able to regain your place in the netball team? For the family, life without you will be very different. They may be wondering how much they can plan for Christmas or for the holidays. They may be particularly embarrassed by the question of how to enjoy good times without you.

Where is the centre of your world? In hospital or outside? In the classroom, at home, or in your relationships with your friends? Where is the centre of your world?

Leaving Hospital

When you come out, do remember to think about whose decision it is. The decision that you and your parents made for you to go in was only possible because of the offer made by the hospital. It is not the same about leaving. The staff may say to you, 'You must go', or they may say to you, 'You must stay.' Remember that it is only the first that has to be obeyed.

Dawn's violin and appendicitis

It was 10 days before Dawn's next violin exam. She was anticipating it with a mixture of dread and excitement. It was an important one on which would hinge the possibility of going on to music school. The violin was an important passion of hers.

That Sunday morning Dawn complained of stomach ache. As the morning progressed the pain became more acute and she vomited. Her parents were understandably concerned and called out their local GP. Such was their expression of concern on the telephone that he came round quite soon, examined her and said that it might just be a stomach upset and they should wait. They could ring him up later in the afternoon if things did not improve.

Dawn kept saying she would be all right and did not want the doctor contacted again. Her parents could see that she was getting worse. They did call the doctor again. He returned and made another examination and said that he thought it was appendicitis and they should get Dawn to the hospital as soon as possible. Dawn protested at this. 'I am not going to hospital. What about my violin exam? I am not going to miss it, and my friends are calling round to see me this evening. I have made arrangements with Julie.'

Her parents said, 'We are all concerned and worried about your missing things that you think are important; but you are important and we are deciding that you have to go to hospital, at least to see what the specialist says.'

They took Dawn, still protesting, in their own car with their GP's letter. She was admitted and, after they had signed the form giving their consent to the operation, she was operated on and her appendix, which was dangerously inflamed, was removed.

Postoperatively Dawn had a good recovery and enjoyed the visits and cards from her friends and the special attention. But she was dying to get back to her violin. She was in an open ward and so had no chance to practise, let alone strength to do so in the first few days. Four days before the exam, when her parents were visiting and expecting to take her out the next day, the doctor said that when they had removed the stitches that morning there had been a small abscess and Dawn's temperature had gone up. She had to stay in hospital for another week.

Dawn heard this news with dismay. Her parents too were concerned about what to do. Dawn said to them, 'Look, I really want to take this examination. If I am not well enough to do it, then I am not well enough, but I feel that I am able if I could be at home to do some practice over the next couple of days. What I have got now is not as serious as appendicitis. I am just ill. I can be ill at home.'

Her parents decided to take her home and they shared this view with the doctor. He said, 'But you can't do that. You must see the consultant. I have said that she has to be in hospital for another week.'

'We have heard your advice, doctor, and thank you for it. We have decided that we shall take our daughter home.'

12

Dying

Like you, we shall die. When this happens, somebody will feel some pain. It is particularly painful for others when someone close dies sooner than expected. Adolescents, too, are at risk of dying sooner than expected. It is often difficult for people to realise that the commonest cause of death in adolescence is violence in its many forms, including accidents. The second most common cause is suicide, and the third most common cause is cancer. We may comfort ourselves by realising that, despite the risks which you adolescents take, on the whole you do not die with such frequency as older people.

Adolescents' Dying

We think that this painful experience is particularly agonising because of the special sense of outrage that is felt when an adolescent dies. A life unfulfilled, a waste. Most parents have at some time the idea that their children may fulfil some things which they themselves did not. This absolutely, simply and totally, cannot be so if the adolescent dies. The parents are cheated of that idea. They lose not just a uniquely loved companion, not just someone that they have nurtured and seen grow, but someone that embodied hope and expectation. And the adolescent loses his or her life.

Ian's funeral

At Ian's funeral the vicar said that he was sure that of all the feelings that most must have in the church that day, the strongest must be the feeling of anger. 'When we go outside to the graveside, we shall throw that anger at God.'

What Jennifer left behind

Jennifer had leukemia and the remissions were getting shorter as the drugs lost their efficiency. The doctors told her parents and they deliberated about how they could deal with this. They had often discussed her condition with her. She was aware of the life-threatening nature of what was happening. Her parents decided that they would say to her that it was clear now that unless a miracle happened, the battle was lost. They did not use the word 'die' but they said to Jennifer that they would like her to think about what she wanted for herself in her last time, and what she would like to do with the remainder of her life. They said they knew they would all have a lot of memories of her after she had gone but wondered if there was something that Jennifer might specially want to give to each of her brothers as a sort of parting gift. Jennifer did choose things for both of them and, unbeknown to her parents, chose gifts for them too.

Her brothers were told, too, and were told that their parents expected that the brothers would have a lot of feelings about it, but because they were young, would not be thinking about it quite so often as the parents would.

It was all right for them still to be interested in their football or their collection of model cars, and to go on playing; but from time to time they would probably have pangs of very strong feelings.

The family were lucky that Jennifer's hospital had a home care team whose task was helping to make it possible for people to die at home. So, with help from nurses and a social worker from the hospital and with her family at her side, Jennifer died at home. At her funeral everybody from her class came; they had sent a special bunch of flowers.

The family had collected many things by which to remember Jennifer. There were photographs, some of her special things and the presents that she had chosen for herself. But they did not keep things obsessionally in a sort of 'Miss Haversham' style, with everything staying exactly as it had been. Indeed, six weeks after Jennifer died, one of the brothers, Andrew, asked if he might now be able to have her room. His mother agreed.

A few things were kept in the house in some obvious places, like mantelpieces and shelves, and some were kept in the drawers where the old photographs and family curios were stored.

Jennifer's parents had attended a group for parents of children with leukemia. They continued to be very comforted by meeting others who had lost children and talked about their experience. They found that they needed more. At work and in their leisure time, they found they needed to talk about what had happened. The children did this too and the parents encouraged them always to remember Jennifer and talk about her. As the months went by they did this, not in a morbid way, but with 'Remember the last time we were here, Jennifer was with us' or 'You know, Jennifer would have liked this' or 'Hey, this reminds me of when Jennifer had that bike'.

The pain never went and still they would find themselves crying; but, as time went on, they got more used to it.

Parents' Dying

The chances are that your parents will die before you do. That is because they are older. We do not know if people are ever ready for this event, but we know that if it happens when you are still a teenager it is especially difficult. Difficult as it may be for you to acknowledge that you are dependent on your parents for one thing or another, you know that you are.

Robin's loss of his father

Robin's father had an accident on a building site where he worked and he was killed instantly. Robin was at home with his mother when the policeman knocked on the door. Robin answered the door and was very surprised that the policeman said he wanted to come in. His mother seemed to sense something in his manner that made her start and say, 'What's the matter?'.

The policeman said, 'I'd like you to sit down.' He said to Robin, 'You stay. I've got some bad news for you.' Then he told them.

His mother started to sob and Robin did not know what to do. He said, 'I'll make a cup of tea.'

The policeman said, 'Never mind about the tea. I'll make it. You go over to your mum.'

Robin went to his mother and put his hand on her and found that she cried as she had never cried before. As well as tea, the policeman asked a neighbour to come in and then he left.

There was so much to do and so much crying to do but Robin could not help the other feelings coming too. He saw that this was the difference between him and his mother. She was in despair all the time and was really dependent on her neighbours' telephoning people, getting in touch with the other relatives, getting food in and helping with the funeral arrangements. He, on the other hand, kept getting all sorts of other feelings coming in, like wanting to get out of the house or wanting to go out with his friends, but when he was doing that he would suddenly get the other feelings back and feel this awful pain inside him and want to go home again. And he wanted to be alone a lot of the time. In his room he started looking at the things his father had given him and the photographs of them together on holiday the year before. He got worried about what he would wear for the funeral and furious with himself for having such a practical concern.

The funeral took place three days later and the relatives descended. Robin found some of it very moving but some of it made him want to scream and yell at them all. One of the things that he felt guilty about was that all these people kept on talking about how wonderful his father was and he kept on having memories about other times when he wasn't wonderful at all. He remembered the arguments.

After the funeral there were practical arrangements to make, but he went back to school. He often talked to his mother about his father and she talked to him and he was sometimes able to talk to his friends. At school the teachers often asked him how he was. They managed not to be patronising or to make less demands on him. They said things like, 'How has it been this week, it is just two months now isn't it?' He realised that they kept it in their minds too.

His mother got back to the business of her work and sorted things out much more slowly than he did and he had to take on a few things in the house. They both had to go on coping with their changed life.

13

Outside Authorities

The Law

You will have been on a car journey or on a bus or walked down a street. You will have done this in a country where things are so organised that all the traffic going in the same direction stays on one side of the road, for that is the rule. It is called the rule of the road and the consequences of breaking it vary from disapproval to death. The consequences covered by the law range from the extremes of a caution at one end and imprisonment at the other. We take it that you are reassured by this and by there being someone who makes sure the rule is kept. We are as well. We agree with you that a police force is necessary.

There are laws about most aspects of people's lives and you live in the sort of society in which it is said that none is above the law. But many laws are widely broken.

We distinguish between breaking laws and not respecting laws. For example, to take motoring again, the speed limits are widely broken. This does not mean that they are held in no respect at all. We have, for example, not come across widespread advocacy for the abolition of all speed limits. Indeed, it is a commonly stated view that while most motorists break the speed limit, they do so only to a certain degree and that if the speed limits were raised, the speeds at which people travelled would be raised by a predictable amount.

No games have no rules. Part of the fun in some games is breaking the rules or going as close to breaking them as is possible, as, for example, playing along the touchline in football. In some games the rules are so complicated, or mutual agreement between the two sides about infringement so difficult to attain simultaneously, that a member of one team or someone outside both teams is given a role specifically to watch over the rule keeping. These people are called umpires or referees. Umpires and referees are also given powers of sanction. In some games they can award penalties which may include banning someone from the game.

Again, we should like to note a distinction between penalties and punishments. We see penalties as simply the legal consequence of infringing a regulation. We see punishments as a formal attempt to inflict physical or emotional pain or suffering on someone who seems to have done morally wrong. We call wishes to do the latter, punitive feelings. And we think all of us have them.

Families and Parents

Parents have been restrained by the law for generations. Fathers, you were not allowed by law to deliver your own child. As soon as your children were born, you had to register them. Then you had to ensure that they were exposed to education. The law said you were not to leave them alone until they were a certain age (do you know what that was?), that you were not to give them alcohol in a public house, that they should not be sold cigarettes under the age of 16, that you should not wilfully injure them.

As parents you are likely to have anxieties sometimes lest your adolescent gets into trouble with the police, at least in connection with motoring.

If you are following our line of thought in this book, you will be with us in seeing all our behaviour as a potential message. Are you aware of the messages or communications which you are giving to your adolescents? Is it that they are not to break the law or is it that they are not to be found out? Or is it something else?

Your children will know if you exceed the speed limit in your car. They will know if you permit them to buy cigarettes when under 16. They will know if you give them alcohol to drink in a public house when they are under 18. They will know if you turn a blind eye to their going too young to certain films or too old on certain tickets for public transport. They will know if you steal from work, if it is clothing, electrical goods, tools, or even if it is only a paper clip or piece of paper or envelope or electricity for photocopying. Note our compromise. We are distinguishing between different levels of theft.

Who is on whose side? It is a common view to see the law breakers and the law enforcers as two sides. They are called 'us and them'. There is another view and that is that there is only one side.

If society is seen as a system, then it is easier to see that everybody is both us and them. It depends from where you look at it. For instance, the head of a primary school may be seen as someone apart or powerful in authority. The head can easily be put into the position of 'them', with the pupils as the 'us' who depend on and resent his authority. But where would the head be if none of his pupils came to his school? He is utterly dependent on the parents of the children sending them to his school by choosing to get them out of bed, to dress them, to pack them off in the morning. In that context he can see himself as the 'us' and the people in authority or the people on whom he is dependent as the 'them'.

Similarly with the different groups of people such as the police. All of us are part of a society that makes certain rules called laws by which we live. We have police forces to make sure we are not breaking those laws and to apprehend those of us who do. Society usually has representatives, like police committees in this country, who have some power over the police. The police then enforce laws and can use their authority in their relationship with us. That can be seen as the police being over us. However, we have decided that we need the police force, and so we are 'over' them. This circular relationship can be either negative or positive, or neither.

You may have many feelings about the police, but it is you who put negative and positive qualities to it. For instance, you may be part of a family that, because of its previous history of law-breaking and involvement with the police, has a negative view of the police. You may feel the police have a down on you. You may also be living in an area which has an authority which has decided that there should be greater local control over the police and therefore your local force feels that the officials whom you have elected have a down on them.

We want to tell you something more about how we see some of the people that you may encounter as upholders of the law. Think about what it might be like to be a policeman, a magistrate, a social worker, a probation officer. Some of them, whom we have met as clients or colleagues, have told us a bit about it.

Court Decisions

How many magistrates, before they make a decision, ask the family what they think should happen? In England and Wales and Northern Ireland at any rate this does not happen very often. In Scotland the system of family courts ritualises such a forum.

There is a gulf between magistrates and young people which is even greater than the one sometimes felt between adolescents and other adults. They are set up to appear different or higher. They often sit up high, behind wooden barriers. They come in through a separate entrance and everybody else is told to stand up while they do so. As people, they often come from a certain section of society and so talk differently from the average man in the street. They certainly come from that section which is called respectable or successful or upstanding. They are the pillars of the community.

You may be bored with our saying so, or feel it is all part of an adult conspiracy when we do say it, but we really have seen another side to them. In our experience in meeting magistrates informally or sitting with them while they do their work, we have found them to have the same doubts, concerns and cares as most people. They find the job of balancing their ideas about the needs of an individual adolescent against the needs of society to be a difficult one. Their experience is that harsh sentences for young people do not have a particularly high rate of success. They are always open to examine ways in which youngsters can remain in the community and, indeed, one of our professional criticisms of them has been that we have felt they sometimes lean over backwards to consider mitigating circumstances. Of course magistrates and judges make decisions that may feel unfair or unjust to adolescents. They do it to adults as well. Like examiners, whom we have already described as trying to pass candidates, we describe magistrates as always trying to be fair. You might find it helpful to think of them in this way as it may then be easier for you to influence them. That, we are sure, you are interested in.

Sometimes they are faced with having to make decisions because they feel society cannot be seen to tolerate particular sorts of behaviour.

Jonathan and what the community would tolerate

Jonathan was 16 and came from what the police described as a respectable, good family. He had behind him a couple of cases of shoplifting for which he had received a fine on the first occasion and a conditional discharge the second.

This time he had been found with two other youths, one younger and one older, stopping cars, brandishing an axe, and demanding money. He was sent by the court to a residential institution whose job it was to give an opinion about what should happen. Jonathan spent three weeks at this place and it was felt by the professional people that Jonathan might well respond to a community service order which would mean some work in the community for several hours each week over several months.

This recommendation was given to the court. The magistrates heard all the evidence, talked with Jonathan in the court about his views and to the family about theirs, heard a very eloquent plea by Jonathan's solicitor that he should continue to receive professional help plus the community service order and listened to the social workers involved.

When they returned with their sentence they said to Jonathan 'We feel that you would benefit greatly from a community service order, Jonathan, and from the important work that has begun between the social workers and your family. However, sadly, we have to say to you that our community just cannot tolerate young people stopping cars with axes and demanding money from people. For this reason we are sending you to a detention centre for three months.'

If either of you, as a parent, or you, as an adolescent, become involved with our legal system, be it magistrates or police, then we suggest you ask yourself, 'How is this a problem to me and what am I going to do about stopping it from being a problem?'

It is a sad fact of life that once you start to break the law you become noticed and the more you are noticed, the less you can get away with. So it is very easy to get the feeling that you or your child is being picked on and being persecuted for things that other youngsters get away with. This is the reality of things. Once somebody is noticed in the community as somebody who breaks the law, then they have a 'high profile' and will be picked up more. Parents, please try to get this through to your children and get them to think about the circumstances and the position which they have put themselves into. Get them to consider the company they keep and the places they frequent.

Gordon and the foreign police

On holiday abroad, Gordon left his parents and sister sunning themselves on the beach and decided to take himself into town, with his mother's parting words of 'Mind where you go' and his father laughing, 'Don't do anything I wouldn't do.' He found himself in the main square enjoying the hustle and bustle. He noticed with interest that a group of people with placards were approaching, chanting slogans, which he could not understand. 'This should be good for a laugh', he thought as he decided to stay around and join in if he could.

The sound of the sirens heightened his excitement, and when the police arrived there was a general mêlée. He thought then that he should try to get out of it, but before he could act he felt his hair being pulled sharply. Instinctively, he turned round and lashed out, hitting the policeman who was doing it.

Inside the police van, Gordon continued to shout that he was British and nothing to do with the demonstration, but the guards and fellow captives all looked on him with hostility.

He was released some hours later but it was only on going home in the taxi with his parents that he realised that he owed his freedom to their intervention rather than to his own defiant protestation. 'Those pigs and the way they treated us – I couldn't do a thing', he said to his father.

His father replied, 'You went into the square; you have your hair below your shoulders and you decided not to wash it. You stayed around and you hit the policeman. They are coming to interview us tomorrow and the rest of us would like to be allowed to spend the remainder of our holiday here.'

More about Courts

Our own view is that it is often in this very attempt to be liberal and kindly that magistrates' courts become very unclear. Often some of their most caring decisions are the most muddling and feel to the adolescent to be the most punitive.

Just like the police and the rest of us, magistrates feel a need to be recognised and respected, and for the process in which they are involved to be taken seriously.

You will be very aware of the importance of appearances and how you judge people by them. You may be a member of a group of friends who all have certain similarities in dress and are keen on particular fashions, looking down on others who dress differently. If you happen to be in the school play or even attending an evening event which your parents attend, and they arrive dressed in, say, a dinner jacket and evening dress, you may feel affronted or embarrassed. So too with magistrates. One of the simplest ways of getting on with magistrates is dressing in the way which they equate with respect, and when you are in court, acting in a similar manner.

Some people we know have found role-playing a helpful thing to do. They have acted going to court, being a magistrate, a policeman, a solicitor and so on.

In our experience, it is important to know which people in your life are important. It may never happen to you but, at some time in your life, magistrates may become very important to you because they are sitting in judgement over you or your child. We should like you to think about what to do to impress upon them that you are at least as committed as they are to avoiding its happening again. If you are a parent this may be the best service that you can do for your child.

And professional advisers have difficult decisions too. They have no way of knowing what is best and have to decide what they are least anxious about.

Wayne's difficult life

Wayne was 15 and lived with his mother, stepfather and two younger brothers. His behaviour had brought him into contact with the police and the courts. What Wayne had done had been to set fire to the school secretary's office after being suspended for hitting a teacher.

So seriously did the juvenile court view this offence that they felt they would remove the case to the Crown Court for sentencing. In the interim, Wayne had been remanded in care to the local authority who admitted him to an observation and assessment centre.

Wayne settled in well. From his first day he took part in the life of the centre, talked engagingly to the staff, was popular with his peers and never argued about doing chores. His family came to visit him and their first informal contact was pleasant, although they were filled with anxiety and worries about Wayne's future. Work with the family and Wayne uncovered a traumatic childhood which included parental and family violence, transient relationships with adults which were mainly rejecting and difficult. The professionals could make many links between what had happened in Wayne's past and his present behaviour which led up to his being where he was. Throughout his time in the centre, Wayne continued to join in fully with all activities, looked and worked on the difficulties he had been in, talked to staff, did well at school and got on with his peers. His family were frank and open about what had gone on in the past and seemed genuinely to want things to change. The professional workers could see many positive areas which could be developed with Wayne and his family in the future.

Prior to his Crown Court appearance, all the professionals involved in the case met to discuss recommendations to the court. These included people from the probation department, social services, education, and staff from the residential centre. All talked very positively about Wayne's experience in the centre, the difference they had seen and the hope for work in the future. They felt that the experience had been so positive that avenues which had hitherto been closed were now open for exploration. Both the family and Wayne were very keen to work with professionals in the future to try to change their patterns.

Plans for a treatment programme for Wayne and his family were being made when one member of the group discussing the case who had remained largely silent throughout said, 'Look, people can't go around setting fire when they have a grudge. I can't think of anything more dangerous.'

With this statement the mood of the meeting changed. The professionals there started to look at the gravity of Wayne's crime. Indeed, society did not tolerate people's setting fire to property or buildings. As responsible professionals, although feeling a conflict of interest over Wayne's future and what was best for him, they had to take as a priority society's safety and code of conduct.

The recommendation was made to court in these terms, although reporting fully on Wayne's positive contribution to the centre and his family's willingness to work.

What do you think should have happened?

The Police – Criticism and Influence

There is a lot of excitement in the police force. Some of it about real events, and much of it about anticipated happenings. But police also have to do policing. It is a job which has to be done, like the job of the referee. Some of it is not very easy because, unlike the rules of most games, laws are sometimes very ambiguous. Policemen or policewomen will see themselves as symbols of authority for society and, because adolescence is often a time of negative feelings towards society or authority, will not be surprised to be taking the brunt of some of those negative feelings.

Forget about them as police for the moment and just think of them as people who have chosen to do a job. No matter how much any of us may profess to value it, none of us likes negative criticism. How would you react if something you had chosen to do was criticised consistently by someone else for half an hour? How would any bus driver get on with his job if the passengers freely advised him about when to overtake, to stop, to go faster, or complained about the price of fares?

Although you may have several negative comments to

make about your school, how it works, or what value it has, imagine someone from another school telling you for half an hour or more all the negative things about you and your school. Even if they are putting forward views that you happen to agree with, you may object to the criticism.

In the BBC television programme, 'Grange Hill', that school was merged with another. Pupils from both schools, previously vociferous in their criticism of both establishments, became indignant when their opposite numbers made any disparaging comment about their particular school.

If your teacher gave you criticisms about your work for half an hour, mentioning only the bad points about it, what would you feel about that and about your teacher, even if you felt that the criticisms were right? Most of us do better when what we do is put in as good a light as possible.

Let it therefore be no surprise that the police are like the rest of us and do some things well and some things badly. Also, like the rest of us, they respond 'badly' to an overdose of negative criticism. Their pride in their work does not have to be interpreted by you as an expression of feelings of superiority and their negative responses to your criticism reinforce how you feel about them.

Probation Officers

Probation officers are officers of the court, but it seems to us that that is what they like least about their job, for they do not like to be seen as just another sort of policeman. In many ways they do similar things to social workers, but there is a difference. They are more concerned with their clients' breaking the law. They are expected to help people to stop committing offences. They may want to focus on why the offending was done, and on changing behaviour. They used to be thought of as a soft option but can now be seen as an alternative option, which may require a far greater commitment than going to prison.

Social Workers

Society has a view about how people should live, and employ social workers to make it feel that it is doing something about this. Social workers have two functions. One is to offer to help people who have difficulties in living in the way that society likes people to live (ie not in poverty, not in distress, not in hardship, not in an insane way). The second function is to be the person who does something when society thinks something should be done. Social workers are the 'something should be done' people. They have powers to arrange money, to influence rehousing, to initiate the removal of children into care, adults into mental hospitals or old people into old people's homes.

They are often asked by courts for reports and to supervise adolescents who have broken the law.

We think social workers are often torn between letting their clients make their own decisions and intervening. By the very nature of their job, their best intentions are often seen as interference.

But, to talk about sides again, social workers like to think that they are 'on your side'. You might find that as a group they most dislike the idea of 'us and them'.

Alan and the court rehearsal

Alan was to appear in court for an offence of drinking and driving on his moped. He had never appeared in court before, and after investigation he discovered that nobody in the family had been to court either. A couple of his friends had been to court for various acts of delinquency but they were not much help in getting the information that he wanted.

The information that he wanted was what it was actually like. Being a keen footballer he knew the advantage of knowing the ground that he would be playing on and the advantage of the home team in knowing their own playing field. He felt that this ordeal would be like playing away from home on a pitch that he knew nothing about.

He decided to see if he could actually visit the court and find out what it looked like. He asked his teacher at school what he could do and she replied, 'Well, just go and see what it is like.' She did tell him where to find out the hours and what to say if he was accosted by anybody in an official capacity, but emphasised that it was a public event and he had the right to go. He was over 16, so school attendance was a bit more flexible than it had been the year before. She expected the courtesy of his letting her know when he would be attending.

Alan made the necessary arrangements and turned up on the Tuesday morning at the local court. The first thing that struck him was the general run-down nature of the building. It looked decidedly seedy, the furnishings were a bit tatty, the decor had obviously not been touched for some time. There was a bit of cardboard over a ventilator, the building was badly in need of repair and a coat of paint. The people hustling about were either policemen in uniform or various other official-looking people with clipboards and files. They were not dressed particularly smartly but had an air of knowing what they were doing and they were talking and joking with each other.

'How can they be joking at such a serious matter,' he thought. 'I'll be here next week and they will be making jokes about me.'

There were other people outside the courtroom, some laughing and seemingly carefree, a lot of people smoking, and others looking as if all the worries of the world were on their shoulders. One young boy, who seemed no older than he, was crying and sobbing in a corner. He was overwhelmed by the awesomeness of it all.

'How can I possibly give a good account of myself in a place like this? With all this bustle and activity going on, everybody looks as though they know what to do and I haven't a clue what I should be doing here next week.'

He went back to the visitors' gallery and sat through a couple of cases. There was somebody who had not paid his telephone bill and was being prosecuted for that; some requests for alcohol consumption licence extensions. As luck would have it, the last case that he sat through was one for drinking and driving. A man had been stopped in his car at 11 p.m. and was found to be over the legal limit. His solicitor put up a very strong case of mitigating circumstances: the man had religious objections to alcohol, but had been given drinks at a work party and his car was essential for his occupation. He got a twelve-month disqualification from driving and a £60 fine.

When Alan went to court the next week he felt infinitely more prepared than he had been for his first visit, but he concluded that court was a place to avoid in future.

14

Leaving Home

Many factors rule the way society operates in influencing the leaving home process. Most people leave home between the ages of 16 and 23 and marriage is by far the commonest reason. Sometimes government taxation and benefit make it economically more viable for 16-year-olds to leave home and set up by themselves, while at other times it is just the opposite. However, it may well be possible that at 16 a young person may not be emotionally ready to leave home at this stage, nor his parents to let go of him or her. Employment is another factor which can affect this process.

Wendy, whose place is it?

Wendy lived away from home, in London, where she was going to university. Her father was a respected professional who held a prominent position in the local community of the small market town where Wendy had been born and brought up. Her father missed her a lot and particularly he missed the impassioned arguments about politics that they used to have. Her mother, on the other hand, joked about how nice it was to have no more arguments.

At Easter Wendy came home for the vacation. On a Saturday morning she went off for what she said was a 'meeting'. That evening in the local news on television Wendy's father was astounded to see her face on the screen. It was a demonstration and there was Wendy in a prominent position, holding a banner. It was confirmed that his eyes were not deceiving him when the local paper dropped through the letter box and there she was on the front page.

That evening when she returned home, he confronted her about her behaviour.

'Dad,' Wendy said, 'you and I have got to agree to differ. We have different opinions about things that are happening in the country today. We are both adults.'

Her father replied, 'I respect your opinions but I object to you demonstrating here where I live and where I work. This is my place.' He angrily added, 'I am not going to be shown up here of all places.'

'This is my place too,' Wendy retorted.

Her father said, 'You don't live here any more.'

'That may be,' said Wendy, 'but this is still home. Are you saying it is not?'

Her father said, 'Of course I am not saying that, you are just twisting my words.'

The atmosphere at home that evening was strained but things changed with a general discussion, one in which her mother also joined, about the state of the world today.

After Wendy had taken herself off to bed, her mother and father were talking about her. Her mother said to him, 'You have got to accept that she has left.'

Her father said, 'Yes, but it is all on her terms. She is still here when she wants to be.'

Mother said, 'Yes, the terms have certainly changed. It used to be, "You be in by 11 o'clock", now it is, "I'll be home at Easter".'

Beverley: what her father feared most

Beverley's father got a message at work asking him to collect her from her work at 6 o'clock. She knew that he could just make it from his office. In fact her father had a cancellation and left early and would have arrived at Beverley's place with 15 minutes to spare if he had not stopped to buy the evening newspaper. As he sat in the car reading it, he wondered why he felt so reluctant to arrive there early.

He remembered the excitement of collecting her from school

when she would run out with all her friends and they would all come up to him. Of course that stopped with secondary school where she seemed to be rather embarrassed by his nearness at any time, but they were getting on better since she left school and got that job. He wondered what it was that he might see or find out if he got there early. What was the worst thing that could be in the back of his mind: that she was in a sexual embrace with a boy or, worse still, an older man; might he find out that her work was messy and that she was not very good at it; might he see her smoking? He decided that the thing that he would find most difficulty in accepting of all those three was seeing her smoking.

He was somewhat shocked at this piece of self-discovery, and mentioned it to his wife later on that evening. She said to him, 'Well, you're lucky, aren't you? Remember you own dad, the most difficult thing he had to face was your marrying me.'

Kevin and Morris dancing

Stan's young son Kevin was very involved with Morris dancing and at an early age had won several competitions. The Morris dancing fraternity predicted great things for him. He was really one of the best young dancers they had seen for several years. Stan and Kevin went all over the country taking part in competitions and festivals.

One day when Kevin was 15, Stan came home and said 'Well, we are off to Worcester this weekend.'

Kevin said, 'I don't feel like doing that. I have something else on.'

Stan was stunned with this and said, 'Well, it is quite an important tournament you have entered for.'

'Well, Dad, I have been thinking about dancing. I'd like to have a rest from it. You see last week my friends saw me down at the local shopping centre when we were doing our exhibition and I really got fed up with their jokes – I've been getting them at school all week and I really think I have grown out of it.'

His father was furious with him and it took him a long time to realise it was something to accept.

Responsibility and Accountability

You have not really let go of your children until you stop feeling you have to rescue them. That is until you stop taking responsibility from them and holding them accountable for what they do.

You may be a bit like the mother who when her teenage daughter tells her she is pregnant says, 'Now my dear, are you sure it is yours?'

Neil and the car keys

After he passed his driving test Neil was allowed to drive his mother's old banger. He kept on losing the keys but it did not matter because his mother and father both had spares.

His parents were fed up about it and were discussing what to do. They realised that Neil did not feel accountable for the vehicle, but they did not feel punitive enough to stop him from using it. Then they had an idea. On the morning of his eighteenth birthday Neil received a box containing all the sets of keys to the banger. He was puzzled at first and then his mother said, 'Don't you see? We have given you the car. It is yours now.'

Marriage

Again we do not want to take sides in the 'Is the institution of marriage deteriorating?' debate. In our professional work we try not to talk about marriages breaking up or breaking down but rather simply ending. On the other hand there really does seem to be no getting away from the fact that the ending of marriage carries with it pain, nor getting away from the fact that the children of divorced parents do, on balance, present with more troubles than those of parents who have not divorced. This being so and also remembering that change is always taking place, we do wish people not to make major commitments and relationships while they are undergoing periods of great change: this includes adolescence. We advise negotiating one change before embarking on another.

Ann and Gavin: early marriage

Ann and Gavin were childhood sweethearts. They went to primary school and secondary school together. They were the first girlfriend and boyfriend of each other. They were engaged while still at school and they married when Gavin started his apprenticeship.

The relationship was of such long standing and both sets of parents felt that the other's was such a good home, that this was a union with familial blessing. It had a sort of inevitability to it with which they all felt comfortable. No one questioned it.

Ann and Gavin had three children, loved by each of them and adored by all four grandparents, but in their early twenties, Ann and Gavin found that they both had changed. They were settling down into being different sorts of people from the ones they had been in their teenage years. Their tastes were different, and particularly their tastes for other people.

Ann no longer had a taste for Gavin and Gavin no longer had a taste for Ann.

Many years later they had both remarried and resettled, but the cost was high.

15

Conclusions

Ethical Issues

All the professionals that a family of an adolescent may come
into contact with, be they doctor, teacher, probation officer,
policeman, social worker or nurse, say that they have ethical
standards which they apply to their work. You probably have
ethical standards as well about how you conduct your professional life and your personal life. It is rare for a month to
go by without someone raising an ethical issue which becomes a
public concern. Some of the more recent have included
abortion, euthanasia, surrogate motherhood. It is also rare
for a month to go by without somebody raising what they call
an ethical issue to do with some aspect of our own work.
When we discuss a particular strategy or an idea we are
asked, 'Yes, but is it ethical?' What then are ethics?

The study of ethics in itself is a completely separate
discipline and many people have written about it. Like most
things we have views about ethics which, it seems to us, are
introduced into particular areas when people feel uncomfortable about something that is going on. They feel uncomfortable because what is being practised or intended would lead
to either disapproval by people important to them or go
against accepted social standards. On the other hand they
themselves might feel disapproving of the action. Some
people feel that there is a being outside them which lays
down codes of behaviour, gives approval, disapproval and
forgiveness.

Ethics are also brought into play when people feel that a certain course of action will get them into trouble. This is what the ethical committees to do with various professions are largely about.

Of course people have different standards and sometimes the standards of one may come into conflict with standards of another. At the moment of writing, a current issue was the ritual slitting of a sheep's throat outside the home of an Iranian diplomat in a London street. This action was seen not just as grossly offensive but something totally unethical by the cultural standards of the host nation. What right had someone to slit a sheep's throat in the streets of this country? If it had been in an Iranian street then it may have been as distasteful to a Westerner, but the issue of the man's right to do it would not have arisen.

Standards serve some purpose in our lives. One of our own is that we are clear about what is our affair and what is not. We try to be clear about who is responsible for what. In our professional capacity we see people who come into contact with us as being responsible for their lives. We try not to take over. We call this stance our ethic because we do not wish to do otherwise and wish others to do the same.

We may have different ethics in our personal lives from our professional lives. In fact we would go on to say that these are two separate areas although they share some common issues. Very often the way that we would deal with others in our professional lives is different from the way we do privately.

Some of the tactics that we have suggested in this book may seem devious. Is this ethical? We ask people what they are most anxious about. Are they more anxious about doing something which people might consider devious, or are they more anxious about the behaviour continuing? If the former then they will not carry out the action that we suggest. If the latter then they might be prepared to give it a go.

The old saying that 'the end justifies the means' is usually given a negative connotation and is seen in a bad light. We do think that sometimes a particular means to an end is pretty awful, for instance, going on hunger strike to attain some political advantage. However, on other occasions we see that means, no matter how seemingly devious or contrary to accepted social standards, are worth using because of the possible positive change that might be the outcome: lying about the intention to devalue the currency to forestall people buying and selling in the foreign exchange markets, for example.

Ranking Problems

In a ranking list of any problems that you feel you have to deal with in your life as parents, where will you put the problems with your adolescents? Is there any difference between the way that affluent parents, with little or no worry about material issues, perceive and approach their problems with their adolescents, and those who have more of a struggle taking care of the day-to-day things that are needed in life? How would you rank, in order of priority the following needs: survival, providing clothing, heating and housing, keeping your job, paying the mortgage or rent, dealing with the bills, hire purchase, coping with your adolescents? We wonder what interest this book is to those who have the first four things that we mentioned as priorities. Would this book be of different interest to them than to people who have to worry about issues to do with survival?

Our view is that very often the more time or space available to notice a problem, the more it becomes a problem. Once it is decided that something is a problem of high priority, very often the solution that is tried becomes part of the problem and increases it. We have addressed this elsewhere in the book (p. 48).

If you are really concerned about what your adolescent child is doing one strategy might be to try to take an overview of that problem. Include that problem with all the others that you have had to cope with and find solutions to in your life. Put the problems in order of priority or severity. Ask yourself what staying power the problem with your adolescent has. Ask yourself the question, 'In five years' or ten years' time, which of the problems that I am concerned with today will still concern me? In five years' time shall I be as concerned about my child as I am about the electricity bill?'

Everybody has problems in life. It is a question of what note we take of them. Worry has a function for all of us. Certain things will be happening in our lives and sometimes we worry about them, other times we do not. Another exercise is to ask yourself, 'This time last year, what was I most concerned or worried about?' Our guess is that as most people do much the same things year in and year out, this time last year you were doing much the same sort of things that you are doing now. But this time last year you were probably also worried about certain things. Just as you are now.

What determines what you are most worried about? What is the longest period in your life that you can remember having experience of not worrying about something? What is the thing you have worried about most and the longest amount of time? And the least?

One of the things we have already mentioned is that if you have managed to sort out the material issues to do with life, either by luck or by hard work, and do not have to worry about survival issues, then you have more time to worry about things to do with your family life in general or the state of the world today. The period of adolescence gives good material for worrying.

Roger: losing his job

Roger had a well-paid job as a company executive. He was provided with a car, good expense allowance and a cheap mortgage. He did not have to pay for his petrol. He drove at fast speeds and used the car for the smallest of journeys. The family ate well and had at least two holidays abroad a year.

The children, because of their parents' particular viewpoint, went to local state schools but also had all the extra tuition in terms of music, horse-riding and computer studies.

Roger did not understand why Jason, who was 14, dyed his hair green and got into trouble at school. His room was a mess, he did not seem to accept his father's authority. This led to many rows. Often Roger would come home to find his wife in tears because Jason had been rude to her and had not listened to what she was saying. He was staying out late at night, his school work was suffering and the family were preoccupied with his difficulties and problems.

This went on for several months. So much so that Roger scarcely noticed the fall in the company's profits and the memoranda that were coming from the head office in New York. To his surprise one day the manager asked him to come into his office. He told him that, sad as they were and despite his department's excellent progress, they would have to let him go because they were cutting down. He would get generous redundancy money of half a year's salary. Unfortunately things like the company car, expense account and credit cards would have to be returned.

That evening Roger returned home, drew the family together and told them the news. He told them that they would have to cut back. He would be looking for another job and was confident that he would get another one pretty soon. His younger daughter Joanna did not seem to take it in much; she was 10. His wife started crying and Jason said, 'If that is all you have got to say, I am going out now, goodbye.' This led to another shouting match between Roger and Jason. 'Look', said Roger, 'I've got something important to say about the family.' Jason said, 'It is your problem, not mine, what can I do about it?' as he went through the door.

Weeks and months went by and Roger still did not get a job. His old contacts did not return his telephone calls and he found that his age of 48 made it increasingly difficult to make a breakthrough.

After four months he met up with an old acquaintance in similar financial circumstances. They decided to pool their resources, to start up their own company.

When he was drawing up the documents with the solicitor, he was asked about his family. He told him what his wife was doing and about the children. Suddenly he remembered that he had not been worrying about Jason for weeks. Yes, Jason's hair was still green but he was not worrying about him.

Neutrality and Decisions

One of the most difficult states to reach is that of being neutral about things, especially about our children or parents. Sometimes about particular issues to do with adolescence the only thing to do is to realise that there is nothing that can be done. Once you have reached that state, even if it is only for a moment or from time to time, we feel that you are then more able to work out a more creative way of dealing with the problem – or at least a solution that has more chance of working. One of the reasons may be that when you are not so worried or concerned about the outcome and you feel there is nothing you can do, it does not matter what you try because you cannot make things any worse. Sometimes when studying a particular problem, the greatest difficulty is to start doing something different. Very often, you may feel that you have tried everything. If you take a closer look at what you have done, you will probably see that what you have done has been the same thing, done in different ways. You might find that things actually improve once you decide that things cannot improve. It is a bit like the old saying of trying too hard. Once we stop trying too hard, things might work out and we can try hard enough.

The Best Light

You may often worry about the decisions you have made. You are also affected by the decisions other people make. How can you deal with this?

We often meet families where they have to take painful decisions and have to suffer the consequences of someone else's. We say, first consider how you are going to make your decision. Will you weigh up all the pros and cons? Will you make use of past experience? Will you think about which outcome will cause you the least or the most anxiety? Which will give you the most or the least benefit? Once you have done this and made a considered decision, you then await the outcome. We also suggest that you do not speculate about what might have happened if you had decided something different.

There is no way of knowing and therefore this is not a very productive way to spend your time. We offer our own strategy which is to view every considered decision which we have made in the past as the best decision. We have found it easier then to deal with the outcome of the decision and to get on with our lives.

Do Things Ever Change?

Do things ever get better? Is it simply that we deal with things in a different way depending on what is happening in our lives at that time? Probably you adolescents will never again be as confident about the way you can influence change in the world and how you would do things differently from adults. You will never again feel as immortal as you do now.

Paul's college reunion

One ex-student had the opportunity of attending the 25th anniversary of the graduation ceremony for his year. He was surprised to see that the welcomer at the reception was an old man. Then he recognised him as the ageing remnants of the young vigorous lecturer in one of the subjects which he studied as a student. 'I don't know if it has happened to you,' the old man said, 'or if it was the same for you,' he continued, 'but when I was young I used to think that when I was older, I would change things. And when I became middle-aged I found that I couldn't. And now that I am old, I wonder if it is the same for you?

Language Changes

Before human beings ever had words for things, those things existed. From the sounds our ancestors made, differentiation and uniformity developed; 'rules' appeared. They are called language and grammar.

They go on changing, changed by new people coming along and gradually varying the rules. Adolescents are part of this process of change, using different construction of sentences, accents and words. Adults, by resisting this, ensure that only the changes that are most forcibly pushed through get into the language. This is a necessary process for a language to stay alive. The languages that do not accept the process are dead.

This can be seen as a metaphor for the adolescent process. Adolescents push for a change in the order; adults by their resistance provide the necessary boundaries in which the change may be most creatively moulded. This could not be done without a generation gap:

The First Experience

In the middle of a family row, Wendy said to her parents:

> You say you can't understand me. Just remember that I'm going through being a teenager for the first time and you are going through being my parents for the first time.

Helpful Reading

Fiction

Russell Hoban, *Ridley Walker*. Pan, 1982.
Sue Townsend, *The Secret Diary of Adrian Mole, aged 13¾*. Methuen, 1982.
Sue Townsend, *The Growing Pains of Adrian Mole*. Methuen, 1984.

Drugs and Altered States

DES and the Welsh Office, *Drug Misuse and the Young: A Guide for Teachers and Youth Workers*. HMSO, 1985.
Institute for the Study of Drug Dependence, *Drug Abuse Briefing*. ISDD Library and Information Service, 1985.
Marilee Zdenek, *The Right-Brain Experience*. Corgi, 1985.

On Adolescence for Adolescents

John Astrop, *My Secret File*. Puffin, 1982.
Molly Cheston, *It's Your Life*. Pergamon Press, 2nd edition, 1984.
Mick Gower, *Starting Out*. Collins Educational, 1984.
Sid Griffin and Jo Salt, *Communicating in Society*. Cambridge University Press, 1984.
Peter Mayle, *What's Happening to Me?* Lyle Stuart Inc, New Jersey and Macmillan, 1975.

William L. Mikulas, *Skills of Living*. University Press of
America Inc, 1983.
Leslie Newson, *Feeling Awful*. A. & C. Black, 1979.
Sue Porter, *Problem Page*. Edward Arnold, 1979.

Relationships

Kathleen Keating, *The Hug Therapy Book*. Comp Care
Publications, 1983.
Janette Rainwater, *You're in Charge!* Guild of Tutors Press,
1979; Turnstone Press, 1983.
Paul Watzlawick, *The Situation is Hopeless but not Serious:
the Pursuit of Unhappiness*. W.W. Norton, 1983.

Sex and Contraception

Dilys Cossey, *Teenage Birth Control. The Case for the
Condom*. Brook Advisory Centre, 1979.
Jane Cousins, *Make it Happy. What Sex is All About*.
Virago, 1978.
Gillian Crampton-Smith and Sarah Curtis, *Sex and Birth
Control*. Longmans, 1983.
Gary F. Kelly, *Learning about Sex*, Barron's Educational
Series Inc, 1977.
Oxford Women's Health Action Group, *Whose Choice?
What Women Have to Say About Contraception*. Oxford
Women's Health Action Group, 1984.
Alayne Yates, *Sex Without Shame – Encouraging the Child's
Healthy Sexual Development*. Maurice Temple Smith, 1978.

The British Medical Association publish a number of topical
titles in their *Family Doctor* series. These are available
from doctors' surgeries, health centres and libraries. Titles
include:
Contraception – Choice not Chance
Sense and Nonsense About Sex
Sex for Beginners

So You Know About Sex – for Twelve Years and Upwards
Teenage Living and Loving.

Study Skills

Edward de Bono, *De Bono's Thinking Course*. BBC, 1985.
Tony Buzan, *Use Your Head*. Ariel Books, BBC, rev.
  edition 1982.

Helpful Organisations

You may know already that there are agencies/organisations to which you are entitled to go for advice or help. These include your local social services department, family doctor, education authority, the police, Citizens' Advice Bureaux. Each of these has contact with specialist resources.

We indicate some of the other organisations that you may find helpful. For our American readers we offer a selection of their specialist agencies.

United Kingdom

Action on Smoking and Health (ASH)
5-11 Mortimer Street
London W1N 7RH   01-637 9843

Al-Anon Family Groups UK and Eire
61 Great Dover Street
London SE1 4YF   01-403 0888 (24-hour service)
Aims to help teenagers with an alcoholic relative

Drugline
28 Ballina Street, Forest Hill
London SE23 1DR   01-291 2341

Drugs Information and Advisory Service Ltd
111 Cowbridge Road East
Cardiff CF1 9AG   (Cardiff) 0222 26113

The Albany Trust
24 Chester Square
London SW1   01-730 5871
Helps with all problems connected with homosexuality

Gay Switchboard
BM Switchboard
London WC1N 3XX   01-837 7324 (24-hour service)

Brook Advisory Centres for Young People
153a East Street
London SE17 2SD   01-708 1234
Gives advice and counselling on sex, contraceptives and
related matters

NORCAP
49 Russell Hill Road
Purley, Surrey CR2 2XB   01-660 4794
An association for 'adoptees' and their parents.

Exploring Parenthood
Omnibus Workspace
39/41 North Road
London N7 9DP   01-607 9647
A group which explores the problems and pleasures of being
a parent

National Children's Home Family Network
85 Highbury Park
London N5 1UD   01-226 2033
This operates a phone-in service for people with family
problems. In addition to the London telephone number,
there are regional and local offices which can be supplied
from the London centre

Kathryn Redway Associates
18 Ellesmere Road
Twickenham, Middlesex TW1 2DL   01-892 8202
This agency runs courses on how to use your head and study
better.

The Samaritans
Head Office: 17 Uxbridge Road
Slough SL1 1SN   (Slough) 0753 32713
There are offices in all large towns and cities, the telephone
number of your nearest one will be found in the local
telephone directory, or Yellow Pages directory

United States of America

National Network of Youth Advisory Boards
PO Box 402036, Ocean View Drive
Miami Beach FL 33140

Self-Help Center
1600 Dodge Avenue, Suite S-122
Evanston IL 60201

Children of Alcoholics Foundation
540 Madison Avenue, 23rd Floor
New York NY 10022

American Institute of Family Relations
4942 Vineland Avenue
North Hollywood CA 91601

National Committee on Employment for Youth
1501 Broadway, Suite 1111
New York NY 10036

National Association on Drug Abuse Problems
355 Lexington Avenue
New York NY 10017

Alcoholics Anonymous
PO Box 459 Grand Central Station
New York NY 10163

Potsmokers Anonymous
316 East Third Street
New York NY 10009

Pills Anonymous
PO Box 473 Ansonia Station
New York NY 10023

Allied Youth and Family Counselling Center
PO Box 401412
Dallas TX 75240

Parent Resource Institute for Drug Education
Georgia State University
University Plaza, Atlanta GA 30303

The Samaritans
802 Boylston Street
Boston MA 02199

National Organization of Adolescent Pregnancy and Parenting
6813 Winifred
Fort Worth TX 76133

Center for Population Options
2031 Florida Avenue NW
Washington DC 20009

Federation of Parents and Friends of Lesbians and Gays
PO Box 24565
Los Angeles CA 90024

One, Incorporated (homosexuality)
2256 Venice Boulevard
Los Angeles CA 90006

Index